D0262096

ERED

30.

22.
17.

EEN

I NS

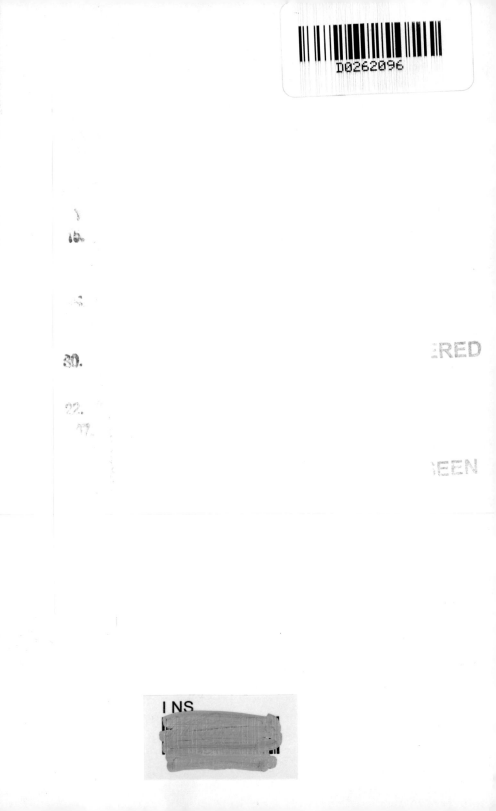

The Vampire Contessa

The Vampire Contessa

From the Journal of

Jeremy Quentain

NORTH SOMERSET
LIBRARY SERVICE

1 2 0468929 8

CHIVERS | 24.3.06

F | £15.99

Marilyn Ross

THORNDIKE
CHIVERS

This Large Print edition is published by Thorndike Press®, Waterville, Maine USA and by BBC Audiobooks, Ltd, Bath, England.

Published in 2004 in the U.S. by arrangement with Maureen Moran Agency.

Published in 2004 in the U.K. by arrangement with the author.

U.S. Hardcover 0-7862-6805-0 (Romance)
U.K. Hardcover 1-4056-3054-X (Chivers Large Print)

Copyright © 1974 by Dan Ross

All rights reserved.

This is a work of fiction. All the characters and events portrayed in this book are fictional, and any resemblance to real people or incidents is purely coincidental.

The text of this Large Print edition is unabridged. Other aspects of the book may vary from the original edition.

Set in 16 pt. Plantin by Christina S. Huff.

Printed in the United States on permanent paper.

British Library Cataloguing-in-Publication Data available

Library of Congress Cataloging-in-Publication Data
Ross, Marilyn, 1912–
    The vampire contessa from the journal of Jeremy
    Quentain / by Marilyn Ross.
        p. cm.
    ISBN 0-7862-6805-0 (lg. print : hc : alk. paper)
    1. Vampires — Fiction. 2. London (England) — Fiction.
3. Large type books. I. Title.
PR9199.3.R5996V33 2004
813'.54—dc22   2004047650

To the memory of Peggy Roth, editor and friend, who many years ago purchased my first paperback novel and who wanted to be part of Jeremy Quentain.

Chapter One

Ominous clouds of yellowish fog wafted up before the young woman in bonnet and cloak who nervously ventured along the bleak Shadwell dock area of London on this night in 1880. Her name was Adele Foster and her normally charming Madonnalike face, was now shadowed with fear. She peered into the thick mist looking for the sign and lights of the Angel Tavern but saw no hint of them.

Turning to her single companion, a hunchbacked old man with a wizened, grim countenance, she said, "I fear we've taken the wrong way, Marlow!"

The old man held up the lighted lantern which he was carrying and also stared into the menacing fog. He was the girl's man-servant and so had accompanied her on this risky expedition into the midnight slums of London's docks.

His rheumy, ancient blue eyes showed a glitter of fear. "It was a mistake to come here, Miss!"

She shook her head impatiently. "No! I

must find my brother and I'm sure he is at the Angel Tavern. He nearly always winds up there on his drunken binges!"

Marlow's thin lips were compressed as he observed in a cracked voice, "That was before, Miss. Things have changed lately. There is no telling where he has gone now!"

Fear deepened on her lovely face. She reached up a hand and nervously touched the black hair which framed her oval face under the wide, yellow straw bonnet. "Don't say such things, Marlow!" she protested.

The hunchback swung the lantern over so that it shone full on her face. "I must say what is true!" he declared.

"You're blinding me with the lantern!" she told him.

"Sorry, Miss." He withdrew it at once.

"I'm sure we can't be far from the Angel," she insisted worriedly as she stared into the foggy night around her.

"We're more than likely to get our throats cut if we tarry here!" Marlow warned her. "I say turn and hurry back out of this mean place as quickly as we can!"

"No," Adele said. "Let us follow the dock down to the right. I think we might find the tavern down there."

"We are in danger of our lives every

minute we delay here!" But he went on ahead, picking his way along the wet, dark stones of the dock in the direction she had indicated.

She stayed close behind him and the lantern. On her right was the harbor with the shadows of ship after ship looming ghostlike in the fog. And to the left were the shabby brick warehouses and tenements: sounds of drunken revelry could be heard from inside many of them.

Adele felt her throat tighten and she drew her thick crimson cloak tightly around her in a nervous gesture. Every so often some figure furtively sidled by them in the foggy darkness. Leering, ugly faces peered at her from the shadows and then vanished. She feared that each such encounter might lead to some unpleasantness, or even an attack, but thus far they had been lucky. These weird denizens of the darkness had been content to pass by, filled with the passion of their own frightening pursuits. She dared not let her mind dwell long on what evil they might be up to. Enough that they prowled by without molesting them!

Yet she was still very much aware of the peril in which she'd placed herself and the trusty old manservant. She had recklessly left her fine West End mansion after the midnight hour when her brother John had not returned. Marlow had hailed a passing cab in which they had ridden until they reached the fringe of the slums, when the irate driver had jerked the vehicle to a halt.

"This is as far as I go," he'd declared. "No man or woman alive would make me drive further."

She leaned out of the cab's window and asked pleadingly, "Not even for a double fare?"

"Not for a triple fare, Miss," the cab driver had told her. "I have me life and me horse and carriage to think of. Though I'll gladly take you back to where we came from!"

She'd grimly descended from the cab and stood in the thick, wet fog. "No," she'd told him. "I'm not turning back. We'll go the rest of the way on foot. Pay the man, Marlow."

Marlow had murmured a few words of warning, but he had gone ahead and paid the driver. That worthy had at once driven off as quickly as he could. She had watched the carriage vanish down the mean street in the mist and felt a sinking sensation. But she hadn't allowed Marlow to be aware of the terror which had assaulted her all at once.

She couldn't reveal her fears without the old man refusing to accompany her. And she needed him!

She'd known that from the moment she'd gone to question her brother's valet. The valet had informed her that John had returned earlier in the evening while she'd been out attending a concert.

"There was a message for him," the middle-aged valet told her.

"Do you know what was in it, Ernest?" she asked.

"I do, Miss," the man said uneasily. "It was a message for him to join Major Merrithew at the Angel Tavern."

Her lovely face had shadowed. "Major Merrithew again! That can only mean an all-night drunken brawl!"

Ernest looked unhappy. "I wouldn't know, Miss."

"It always has before," Adele said sternly. "Major Clare is one of the Contessa's friends and a very bad influence on my brother."

"Please don't tell Mr. John that I let you know, Miss," the valet begged her.

She gave him a disdainful look. "You may be sure I won't. If my brother by some chance comes back while I'm gone, don't tell him of my errand."

"Just as you wish, Miss," the valet said deferentially.

She'd then hastened to don her bonnet and cloak, and find Marlow, the oldest and most trusted of all the servants employed in the fine three-story house. Marlow had come with her and her Johnny to London after the death of her mother in New York. Her father, who had made a fortune in mining, had died many years earlier, so that she and her younger brother were left to share a huge fortune. At her brother's suggestion they had come to live in England for a while. She had not known then that his main purpose in wishing to come to London was to pursue the Contessa Maria! Had she known she would never have given in to his constant urging. But she hadn't realized and so had gladly agreed that they should take up residence in London.

It had been her hope that Johnny, a wild young man, would improve when they came to live in London. This had been one of her main reasons for agreeing to the idea. Her brother had taken so much of her time she'd had little life of her own. Her one romance had been broken because Johnny had disapproved of the man and had remained in a drunken state during most of the period of her engagement. Sadly she'd given in to her spoiled brother and given the young man back his ring.

She was now twenty-five, and Johnny a year younger. At twenty-four most young men had decided on their life's work or profession but there had been no disposition on his part to do so. He had barely managed to get through college, not because of a lack of brilliance, but because of his dissipations, and he was now living the life of a wealthy young man about town without giving a thought to anything else.

Johnny's love affairs had been too numerous to mention, and those were only the ones she knew of. Doubtless there were scores of others. But none of the girls whom he'd known had cared to accept the role of his wife. Or at least, none of the acceptable ones. Adele had thought that perhaps he might find some suitable young woman in London and marry her.

Instead he had met the Contessa Maria! But she didn't even dare think of that sinister woman at this time of terror. As she moved along in the menacing fog with the old hunchback lighting the way with the lantern's sickly, yellowish glow, she did not dare to dwell on the worst of all her fears. Just now she wanted to find Johnny and part him from his drunken companion, Major

Merrithew. He usually returned with her without any argument, and she did not want him in the company of the Contessa's dissolute friend.

A new concern swept through her. Suppose Johnny had not gone to meet the Major, but the Contessa Maria, somewhere else? It would mean she had taken all these risks to no purpose, had come to this dark, underworld section of London on a fool's chase! But Ernest had seemed certain Johnny had been summoned to the Angel Tavern by the Major. She would have to pray that he had informed her correctly.

"Ahead, Miss!" Marlow said suddenly in his cracked voice.

"The Angel?"

"Yes," he replied and indicated with a gnarled finger. "You can see the outline of the sign high above the entrance."

"I see it," she agreed. And so she did. And now you could also see the dull glow from the tavern itself. Its many-paned windows were thick with dirt but some light managed to emerge.

Marlow slowed his gait and gave her an urgent look. "You don't plan to go into that place, Miss?"

"I have done so before," she told him.

"It's no place for a lady like yourself," Marlow protested. "Let me go in and try and find Mr. Johnny."

"He'd pay no attention to you."

"Let me see first if he's there!" Marlow urged her.

She gave him a placating glance. "No. I'd be in equal danger waiting alone outside. Let us go in together."

"It's a rough place!" Marlow worried.

And the shouted oaths and drunken laughter which could now be heard from the tavern with the unlikely name confirmed his words. But it did not change her intentions.

She had entered this boisterous tavern, whose clientele were mostly rough, underworld characters, before, in search of Johnny. But this time she felt more fearful than on those other occasions. It was later for one thing and the noise from the place indicated that it must be more crowded than on those other nights. She let the hunchbacked Marlow lead the way, the lighted lantern still in his hand.

Following him into the Angel's dimly lighted interior, she was met by the thick fumes of cheap gin and tobacco smoke. The few gas lamps offered completely inadequate lighting and the place was crowded so that one had to elbow through towards the bar. She followed the old hunchback who was greeted with loud cries of derision and abuse by the drunken derelicts.

Marlow paid no attention to the shouts and she kept close behind him, not daring to look to left or right. A hand reached out for her and a young tough thrust his coarse, grinning face close to hers.

"You're a likely filly!" was his greeting.

She drew back from him. "Don't come near me!" she cried in reaction.

The coarse one guffawed and so did his mates. She began to share the general derision of the clientele with the unhappy old Marlow. She kept close to the hunchback, her heart pounding with fear as the derisive comments went on. Then she saw Johnny standing at the back of the tavern with Major Merrithew.

Her younger brother was a big man and still handsome, though there was a hint of weakness in his face. Major Merrithew was older, red-faced and arrogant-looking, with a thin, black mustache. Johnny saw her and at once made some comment to the older man. Then he left him to make his way towards her.

Before he could cross the crowded room to reach her a derelict whose black spectacles suggested that he was blind clutched at Adele and with loud laughter gropingly drew her to him to be kissed. She screamed and fought for release while the onlookers shouted and roared with laughter at this new diversion, encouraging the blind man in his assault on her.

Marlow swung around and taking in the situation thrust his crippled but sturdy old body between them so that Adele was freed. The blind man staggered back with a snarl and an oath on his lips. At the same instant the hunchback hurled the lighted lantern directly at him so that it struck him fully across the chest and then bounced down onto the stone floor. It smashed on the floor with the oil spilling and a billowing flame shooting up from it.

The derelicts at once began to panic and crowd away from the flaming lamp and towards the door. Adele lost sight of Marlow in the din and confusion. She felt herself literally swept towards the door amid a mass of stinking humanity. A moment later she was conscious of a hand roughly seizing her by the arm and shoving her in a side direction and away from the main current of the panicstricken occupants of the tavern.

"This way!" The words were shouted in her ear by her brother.

She allowed him to propel her along without any resistance, and found herself going out by a hidden door behind the bar which led to the alley behind the building.

Johnny let go of her arm and said, "What made Marlow do a crazy thing like that?"

She stood there in the damp darkness, feeling weak. "The blind man attacked me!" she said.

"You shouldn't have come to such a place!" Johnny said angrily.

"Where's Marlow?"

He glanced back at the building. "Serve him right if he's trampled on in there. He caused the panic!"

"Don't say that!" she protested.

Her brother gazed down at her through the shadows. "Did you come down here again to get me?"

"Yes."

"You should have known better! I can take care of myself!"

"Not with that Major," she protested. "I was sure you'd get in some awful trouble."

"The Major's all right!"

"He's a friend of that dreadful Contessa's," Adele reminded her brother.

"And there's nothing wrong with her either," was her brother's reply. The noise of the tavern patrons issuing out into the street

18

was filling the night air around them. "That crowd is making a lot of noise about little," was his disgusted comment.

"Will the place burn down?"

"No. They were getting the fire out as we left," Johnny said. "The flames didn't get beyond that spot on the floor!"

"I'm glad," she said with a relieved sigh.

"If they get their hands on Marlow it won't go well with him," Johnny said, pressing against the wall in the alley and peering out into the foggy street in a nervous fashion.

"I hope he's safe!"

"We have no time to worry about him," her brother said tautly. "I want to get you out of here and promptly."

"I can't leave without him," she whispered.

"You'll do as I say," her brother snapped harshly. "Most of them are out of the way. We can make a break for it now!" He seized her by the arm again and literally dragged her out in the direction of the street.

She was swaying on her feet and in no condition to battle with him. She weakly let him lead her. As soon as they reached the cobblestoned street he rushed her away from the Angel. A handful of the derelicts were standing outside the place still. On seeing them they let out annoyed cries and it seemed they might try to follow, but they didn't.

When they were a street or two away from the tavern Johnny halted again and breathlessly said, "This is the end! I will not have you probing into my private activities any longer!"

She gave him a pleading glance. "I only want to do what is good for you. The Contessa and the Major are plainly out to ruin you!"

"That is a lot of nonsense!" he said with some anger.

She saw the grim expression on his handsome face and bemoaned the fact that he had come under the power of the Contessa and her henchmen.

"I won't argue about it here and now," she said.

He looked around in the foggy darkness. "Didn't you come down here in a carriage?"

"Yes. But he would only come so far. We paid him and he drove away!"

"Fine thing!" Johnny said with disgust. "It's worth our lives to work our way out of here to where we can find a cab!"

"It was your misdeeds brought me here!" she told him. "The time I did not come for you I recall you were gone for two days and nights and brought back beaten and near death!"

Her handsome brother eyed her impatiently. "The Major and I ran into thugs. It was no fault of his. Nor any cause for alarm. I survived it!"

"Only because they brought you to me," she said. "Had I not been there to nurse you back to health it might have been a different story."

"Nonsense!"

"It is so," she insisted despite her fear and feelings of misery. "Why does that Major have to frequent such obscure taverns?"

"He had business down here."

"Which means he consorts with thieves," she said unhappily. "That is all you find down here!"

"Shut your mouth!" her brother said. And he roughly thrust her close to the old building by which they were standing. "Someone is coming!"

She said nothing but did as he ordered. Pressing close to the damp wall of the building and scarcely daring to breathe in her terror, she stared off into the fog. Gradually the figure advancing towards them became more distinct and she at once felt some relief.

"Nothing to fear," she told Johnny. "It is Marlow!"

"So it is!" he agreed with a kind of disgust. It was clear that Marlow was far from in his good graces at the moment.

The old hunchback came hobbling up to them and doffed his stovepipe hat. "They turned on me and near killed me!" he gasped.

Johnny gave him a look. "You seem all in one piece. I doubt that you deserve to be after your foolish action in hurling that lantern!"

"I had no choice, Mr. Johnny!" the old servant said plaintively.

"I should not blame you," Johnny admitted. He glanced at her. "It is my sister whom I have to thank for bringing you down here tagging after me!"

"That is true," she said staunchly. She was not going to be browbeaten by him.

Johnny said, "Let us get on our way and keep close together. We will walk for ten minutes through these back streets before we'll reach a place of comparative safety."

She knew this was all too true. Without further words they began their journey back to the more civilized section of the old city. The fog remained as thick and sinister as before and without the lantern the shadowed streets held more threat. She remained between her brother and the old hunchback, grateful that Marlow had escaped with nothing worse than a few bruises.

She could not help but speculate on what had happened to the red-faced Major Merrithew. It seemed certain that he'd not suffered in the melee. He was known to the underworld characters down there and was perhaps the leader of some of them. They would be bound to protect their own. Johnny didn't seem to be in any way worried about his missing companion.

They reached what seemed like a dead end; then she saw there was a small alley on the left, little more than a narrow passage between two old buildings, through which they must pass single file. As they made their way along its black, fetid length she began to feel fear again and she had to struggle not to cry out some sort of urgent warning to Johnny.

They emerged into a mean little street with a single gas lamp at the far end. Its aspect was sinister, and as they quickly made their way along they passed derelicts sleeping huddled on the steps of the rickety buildings. But it was better than the dark passage which they'd so recently braved.

Just as they reached the corner with the

glowing gas lamp on its black iron post two burly figures sprang out of an alley at them. She screamed and Johnny quickly faced the attackers. Old Marlow, battered as he was, stood firmly beside his young master. Then Adele suddenly realized the thugs had most unusual weapons.

The first one came straight up to Johnny and opened his left hand to hurl a round, leaden ball at him. The ball struck Johnny on the right arm and sent him staggering. As he did the attacker retrieved the ball on a cord to which it was attached and prepared to hurl it again.

The other thug was using the same tactics and weapon on Marlow. He was the more successful, for the first blow of the leaden sphere sent Marlow to the ground. The thug knelt by him and quickly began ransacking his pockets. When he finished he leapt up and came towards her with an evil expression on his ogre's face.

"Your purse!" he rasped, his fist holding the leaden sphere ready to be hurled at her.

She reached inside her cloak and produced the purse she'd been carrying with a few pounds and some silver in it. This she tossed to him. He deftly caught it and seemed about to assault her anyway. She screamed and backed away from him.

By this time Johnny had won the battle with the other thug who lay stretched out on the cobblestoned street. Johnny now raced over to the ruffian menacing her and received the sphere directly in his chest for his effort. Johnny staggered back with a look of pain on his pale, bloodied face. Then he roared like a young lion and came back at his opponent.

The second thug, seeming to believe that discretion was the better part of valor, quickly turned and fled down the street to vanish in the narrow black passage which they had just braved.

She cried to Johnny, "Let him go! He may have a knife!"

"Are you all right?" her brother asked, coming over to her.

"Yes. He took my purse but that doesn't matter. What about Marlow?"

Johnny grimly turned and went over to the old man. Marlow was just lifting himself off the street and Johnny assisted him. The old man looked around him in a dazed fashion. "My hat?"

"Your hat!" Johnny said with derision. "You are lucky to still have a head!"

The old man saw his hat and hastily retrieved it and brushed it a little before placing it on his bald head. By this time

Johnny was urging them all along. They hurried on, leaving the one thug still on the ground, unconscious.

It took another five minutes of precarious progress through the mean streets of the slums before they emerged to a more respectable area of the city. And it was another five minutes until an empty cab came clattering up to them and they all got into it.

As the vehicle rattled over the rough streets towards their London house, Johnny studied Adele with an annoyed look. She was seated across from him, next to a silent and forlorn old Marlow.

"I hope you may have learned a lesson tonight," was her brother's comment.

"I could well say the same thing of you," she replied. "It was your madness in going to that place which led me there."

He asked, "How did you know where I was?"

Warily, she told him, "When you did not return, I guessed. I knew that was where you had come to harm before."

"And so you decided to come after me?"

"Yes," she said. "I knew the place from my other visits. But I soon realized this was different. It was much later and much more dangerous because of this."

"We have all come to realize that," he said

grimly, his cut face bearing witness to his words.

"I'm sorry you were hurt," she said. "But I still blame you. I might have been killed trying to rescue you."

"You did not rescue me!" he snapped indignantly. "You and this old fellow merely created a riot in the tavern. You brought on most of the troubles we had. I warn you, do not come after me again. I will not leave with you or help you as I have tonight."

"You mean to see the Major again?"

"Yes."

"And the Contessa?"

"Yes." His tone was grim.

"You must be mad!" she said. "You know what is being said about her!"

Johnny frowned at her across the cab's shadowed interior. "Must we discuss this in front of a servant?"

"I do not mind Marlow," she replied.

"I do," he said.

"What they say of the Contessa Maria is not a secret," Adele protested. "They claim she has been responsible for the deaths of two men to gain their fortunes. You could so easily be the third on her list!"

"That is nothing but wicked gossip!" her brother said.

"I think it is true," she insisted. "And

there is more in addition to that. There are those who say she has evil powers. That she dabbles in Satanism and may herself be touched with the supernatural!"

Johnny laughed harshly. "You must be dreaming aloud to say such mad things!"

"Because she is a great beauty and has the wiles of all wicked women you are blind to her true nature and the danger she represents for you!"

"Calm down, little sister," Johnny chided her. "You would do better to enjoy the pleasures of London's night life yourself than to condemn me. Isn't it about time you found yourself a husband?"

"Now who is taking liberties before the servants?" she demanded.

He laughed again. "Why not, since you began it?"

Hotly, she replied, "I might have found a husband and settled down to a normal married life if I had not been burdened with you. You have kept me too busy taking care of you to allow me any life of my own!"

"On the contrary," her brother replied. "It is you who keep interfering with *my* life!"

The argument between them was a familiar one and might have gone on had they not at that moment arrived in front of their house. Johnny saw her safely out of the carriage and paid the driver. Marlow stepped down into the street stiffly and hastened to open the door for them to enter the large entrance hall.

As soon as they were safely inside the old man closed the door and turned to Adele. "Will you need me any longer, Miss?"

"No, Marlow," she said. "You can go. And thank you for all the risks you took in my behalf tonight."

"Pleased to do it, Miss," the old hunchback said.

Johnny glared at the old man. "Do it again and I promise you I shall dismiss you!"

"Yes, Mr. Johnny," the old man said humbly. And he turned and hastened away to the servants' quarters.

When he had gone Johnny said, "I want no more interference on your part, sister."

"I make no promises," she said.

He hesitated by the wall night-light at the foot of the stairs for a moment. "If you persist, I shall move to bachelor quarters of my own."

She gave him a frightened glance. "You wouldn't!"

"I might," he warned her. "I happen to love the Contessa and I must have my freedom."

Her eyes met his with fear in them. "I did

not dare say it before Marlow. But you know what the whisperings are about her! Some people claim that she is one of the living dead, a vampire!"

Johnny's reaction was to smile at her bitterly. "You must know how silly that sounds!"

"People do believe it!" she said tensely.

"How can you talk about Maria this way?" he said. "You have never even met her!"

"You will not let me meet her!"

"She doesn't want it," he said. "She is a sensitive person and does not care to meet many strangers."

"A lame excuse," Adele said as they went on up to the next floor.

Adele said goodnight to Johnny, who made no reply but stalked on through the shadows in the direction of his room. She stood for a moment watching him fearfully. He was growing to hate her as he came more under the influence of the Contessa. He only blamed her for tonight, rather than being grateful that she had risked her own welfare for his. They would never be the same with each other again.

She opened her bedroom door and stepped inside. And the very moment she did she knew a sudden thrust of terror. She stared ahead of her in the shadows and was convinced that she was not alone in the room. Something or someone was here waiting for her!

Chapter Two

Frozen with fear, she stood in the darkness of her bedroom waiting for some other sound to confirm her suspicions that someone else was there. All was silence for long minutes, and she relaxed enough to hurry across to the dresser and quickly touch a match to a candle there. As she did so she heard the peculiar rustling sound once again, and it seemed to come from somewhere above her near the room's ceiling!

Seizing the candle, she whirled around with a terrified expression on her lovely face. Her eyes scanned the threatening shadows of the big room as she searched for the intruder. And then without warning it swooped down at her from the darkness! A bat larger than her hand! It came threateningly towards her and she screamed and bent down to escape it. The macabre creature swooped up in the air again and circled before coming her way for a second time.

Screaming, she stumbled alongside the dresser and in a flash of quick thinking she groped over the surface until her hands touched a crucifix with a chain which had been given her by a friendly priest and which she often wore. As the bat came diving at her she held up the crucifix and cried out at it to go away. She was near fainting and could not expect her ruse to work, but strangely enough it did! The bat veered to the side and she heard its body thud against the wall before it went swooping back to escape by a small window at the other end of the room which had somehow been left open.

The moment the frightening thing escaped out the window she ran and pulled the sash down. The crucifix was still in her hand and she looked down at it with a feeling of gratitude. Then she leaned against the wall, trembling and sobbing. It was a delayed reaction to the shockingly macabre experience she had undergone. She was still sobbing when there came a loud knocking on her bedroom door.

This roused her out of her upset state and she went to the door and opened it to find her brother standing there with an irate expression on his handsome face. He had removed his jacket and tie and stood there with his shirt open at the neck.

"Did I hear you screaming?" he asked her.

"Yes."

He frowned. "Why?"

She sighed deeply. "When I came into the room I was attacked by a bat."

"A bat?" His tone was incredulous.

"Yes."

"You must have imagined it," he told her. "How could it get into the room?"

"A window had been left open. It left the same way."

Johnny looked anything but convinced. "It may have been a small bird or perhaps one of the large bugs which show themselves in the spring. I can't think it was a bat!"

"I knew you'd refuse to believe me," she said.

"It's not that I don't want to believe you," he replied. "But the chances of a bat being in a city area like this are very small. I'm sure it was a tiny bird and you were foolish enough to let it terrify you."

Quietly, she said, "Whatever you like."

He saw the crucifix in her hand. "What are you doing with that?"

"I used it to protect myself from that thing," she said in a taut voice. "The crucifix drove it away!"

Her brother looked more annoyed. "More nonsense!"

"It's true!"

His eyes studied her coldly. "You are deliberately trying to make more of this than you should!"

She met his gaze resolutely. "I know that sacred objects are useful against such night creatures. You must know that vampires can turn themselves into bats at will!"

"I'll hear no more such talk," he warned her. "If you are all right I'll leave you to go to your bed."

"I'm safe enough now," she said.

"Very well," her brother replied curtly. "Goodnight! I'd forget all about the incident if I were you."

She made no answer to that as he gave her a significant look and then went over to the door and out into the corridor. He closed the door after him and left her alone with the candleholder in one hand and the crucifix in the other. He had known what she was hinting at when she brought up the subject of vampires and he had not wanted to listen to her.

She placed the candle on the table by her bedside and looped the crucifix around her neck. She would continue to wear it. Having made this resolve she began to undress for bed. And while she went about this she debated what the eerie advent of the bat in her room might mean.

It had not been long after Johnny had established a close friendship with the exotic Contessa Maria Fillipio that she'd begun hearing strange tales about the mysterious foreign beauty who had taken up residence in a fine town house near Hyde Park. It was said that she had come to the great city to appear in the opera, but she had so many affairs with men of wealth that there had been no time left for her to embark on her musical career.

During the several years she'd lived in London she had been extremely close to a Lord Darlington who had been found dead under strange circumstances. To make it even stranger, the young man had left her a huge share of his estate in his will. He had been found lying in a courtyard at the rear of his great mansion apparently dead of a heart seizure. It was said that an expression of extreme horror had been registered on the face of the dead man and the only marks on him had been two tiny punctures on the side of his neck. It was thought these had come from the thorny hedge against which he had fallen.

These facts were noted but nothing much was said about his death. The Contessa's manager, a swarthy, rather arrogant man, had been on hand to look after his employer's interests when the will was read.

There was only a little talk until the Contessa's name became linked with that of another prominent personage, William Plowright, the wealthy industrialist.

This was a May and December romance which created a great deal of gossip. Once again the Contessa was seen in public. The stout and choleric William Plowright appeared to dote on her until he was found dead sitting up in his bed. The servants who found him claimed that he was staring straight ahead with a grim expression of horror on his purple face. When his body was being prepared for burial it was casually noted that he also had two tiny punctures at the side of his neck. The undertaker suggested the marks might very well be the result of insect bites.

But when the magnate's will was read and the Contessa once again inherited a large share of a sizable estate, tongues began to wag. The weird circumstances of the two men's sudden deaths became a subject of whispers. And in due time there were rumors that the Contessa was a vampire! One of the living dead who come to life only at night and feast on the blood of their victims. No one could recall ever having seen her in daylight and this fitted in with the gossip since vampires generally were known to sleep in their coffins in the daylight hours.

Of course many people disputed the rumors. Many simply did not believe in the existence of vampires. But those who did kept the rumors alive. Weird stories were told about the Contessa being seen in lonely graveyards after midnight. And it was said that her manager Carlos had been a former lover of hers who now dedicated his life to her in her strange existence.

Adele had heard these rumors soon after she and Johnny had come to live in London. In the beginning she had discounted them as mere gossip. But when her handsome brother had been attracted to the Contessa and began spending all his time with the mystery woman and her friends, such as Major Merrithew, Adele began to worry that the rumors might be true. And that Johnny might have been chosen as the Contessa's next victim!

She had gone directly to Johnny with her fears and he had laughed at her. He was too much in love with the sinister beauty from Italy to hear anything bad said against her. And he claimed the vampire rumor was a crazy one built on the fact that she had once played such a character in an opera. He assured Adele she had nothing to fear. But this had been months ago and Johnny had since come gradually more and more under the influence of the Contessa and her friends.

Several times his extended drinking binges had nearly resulted in his death. And as a result of this Adele had taken to trying to find him whenever she knew he'd gone somewhere with the Major or other of the same circle of drinking cronies. Tonight she had made a third dangerous excursion to the dockside tavern known as the Angel and it had nearly resulted in disaster for all of them.

And this incident of the bat in her room only made her more ready to accept the horrifying story that the beautiful Contessa could transform herself into a bat at will! Had the creature in her room been the Contessa, ready to attack her? It was not beyond the realm of possibility. Even if the Contessa should persuade Johnny to name her in his will and then become her next victim there was the matter of Adele being in the way. Adele saw that unless she were also eliminated, the Contessa could not get the family fortune. So she could believe that she was in as much danger from the evil woman as Johnny.

All these thoughts raced through her mind as she slid between the cool, almost damp sheets of her bed. Her right hand touched the crucifix and she felt some reassurance. And as she stared up into the darkness she knew that she must take some action to save herself and her brother or they must surely die through the machinations of the Contessa Maria. But what to do? That question troubled her until she fell into an exhausted sleep.

She awoke in the morning as the maid entered her room with a jug of hot water. Sitting up in bed, she asked the girl, "What is the weather this morning?"

The maid placed the hot water jug on the commode and said, "It is raining, Miss."

"I thought it was very bleak and gray," she said.

"It is raining very hard, Miss," the maid assured her. She was a young girl with a rather frightened manner.

"Has Mr. Johnny been down to breakfast?"

"Yes, Miss. He has had his breakfast and he ordered the carriage."

"Oh?" She at once wondered where her brother might be going so early in the day. He usually didn't leave the house until afternoon or later.

She quickly went about her morning toilet and dressed. By hurrying she arrived downstairs just as Johnny, in topcoat and homburg hat, was leaving. He eyed her with some annoyance.

She asked him, "Where are you off to so early?"

"The country," he said. "I'm going to visit a friend of the Major's who is said to have a fabulous collection of guns. It's a distance out of town so I'm getting an early start."

"Then you'll be using the carriage all day?"

He shrugged. "I'll send it back if there are other carriages there and I can be sure of transportation. Otherwise you can get a cab if you need to go somewhere."

"I see," she said. "Where is this country place?"

"Not far from the city," he said. "In the direction of Windsor but not all that distance. There's no need to be concerned."

She gave him a knowing look. "I'm always concerned when I know you are with the Major or any of those people!"

"You're being stupid and prejudiced," he told her. "Let us not argue about it anymore." And he left.

She stood by one of the front windows and watched as he stepped up into the carriage and was driven off into the windswept, rainy morning. Bleakly she turned away and found herself facing Marlow. The old man wore a grim expression on his wizened face.

"Do you feel any the worse for last night's experience?" she asked him.

"My shoulder aches, Miss," was his reply. "Other than that I am all right."

"I'm glad," she said. And with a sigh she added, "My brother has just gone out again."

"I know, Miss," the old man said in a sympathetic tone.

"I'm sorry we ever came to England, Marlow," she said. "It seems an age since our happy days back home."

"Yes, Miss," he said quietly.

"I cannot let him go on like this," she worried. "I must find a way to save him."

"I hope so, Miss," the old manservant agreed solemnly.

"I will want a cab after breakfast," she told him. "I'm going into the city. I'm determined that I will somehow do something for Johnny. Have the cab here at ten-thirty."

"Very well, Miss," Marlow said.

She went in to her solitary breakfast and debated what she should do. The family lawyer in America had referred them to a prominent solicitor in London when they had made the voyage across the Atlantic.

But he was an old man who only visited his office a few times a week and would be no use to her in a situation of this sort. Also, she did not feel like asking his advice in the matter. It appeared she would have to find someone younger and more energetic on her own.

As soon as she had breakfasted she changed into a suit of gray woolen material which seemed right for the unpleasant day. She had a small gray hat festooned with tiny flowers to match and over the suit she wore a rain cloak. When she went down to the front door Marlow had the cab there waiting for her.

The driver asked her where she wished to go as he helped her into the closed vehicle. She gave him the name of a short street in the district of the Temple which she knew held the offices of a great many lawyers. She had no particular one in mind and would have to make a chance selection. Now that she was faced with this task she found herself becoming nervous. But she knew she dare not give up her plan. It seemed her one hope now.

The rain continued as they traveled over the cobblestones until they were finally in the short street with its many shabby brick buildings with dark signs featuring gold lettering beside the front doors of each. She leaned forward so that she could look out the window of the cab and study the signs. The cabby, who was seated outside at the rear of the cab, opened the tiny window and spoke to her.

"Where do you want to be let off, Miss?" he asked.

"Right here will do," she said, ashamed to tell him she'd not decided on any particular address.

He halted the carriage and came and helped her down to the street. "Do you wish me to wait?" he asked.

"Not in the rain," she said. "I'll get another cab later. I have no idea how long I may be here."

Having settled this she turned from him and hurried up the steps and into the vestibule of the nearest building. Not until she was in the vestibule did she look at the inside plates with the names of the law firms on it. The first one she read indicated an office on the ground floor. The name of the firm was Oglethorpe and Heustiss, which seemed eminently respectable; underneath in smaller letters was the word *Solicitors*. For no reason she could name she decided that she would try this firm.

Opening the second door which led directly into the dark old building she made her way along a hallway until she came to a door with the firm's name lettered on it. Hesitantly she knocked on the door and then waited.

After a short while the door was opened by a stooped old man with a bald head and sandy sidewhiskers. He peered at her short-sightedly and said, "Yes, Miss?"

Her heart sank. She visualized another firm of ancient partners. But she felt she must at least make a show of interest. She said, "Could I speak to Mr. Huestiss?"

The ancient with the sandy sidewhiskers showed surprise. He informed her, "Mr. Huestiss died near ten years ago."

"I'm sorry," she said. "I must have meant Mr. Oglethorpe."

The stooped one frowned. "Mr. Oglethorpe is in court this morning. But his nephew Mr. King is here. Could he be of help to you?"

Relieved to hear there was a young man associated with the firm she quickly said, "Yes! Please let me talk with him."

"Who shall I say, Miss?" the old clerk asked.

"Miss Adele Foster," she said. "I'm an American so it is very unlikely that he will have ever heard of me."

"Yes, Miss Foster," the old man said. "If you will come in and have a chair I'll enquire whether Mr. King can see you."

She entered the cheerless outer office with its high desk and stool for the clerk and sat in a plain chair, one of several set against the wall. There was a copy of *Punch* on one of the chairs and she took up the humorous magazine and skimmed through its pages as she waited.

After a few minutes the stooped clerk returned and said, "Please follow me, Miss Foster. Mr. King will see you."

She thanked him and rose and followed him down a short, dark hallway which led to a small private office with a rolltop desk, swivel chair and several plain chairs. A blond young man with a pleasant round face stood by the desk smiling at her with boyish interest. He extended his hand.

"How do you do, Miss Foster? Please sit down." He indicated a chair. Settling himself in the chair opposite her he clasped his hands across his fawn vest and waited for her to say something.

In the presence of the young man she found herself speechless and embarrassed. And yet he was so patently sympathetic in his attitude that she knew it was nonsense to feel as she did. She was sure this slender young lawyer would turn out to be the person she so urgently needed.

Leaning forward a little in her chair, she said, "I have come to seek help for my brother."

"You are American," the young man smiled. "Higgins said you were. Your accent is delightful."

She blushed. "I think your English accents most admirable."

"Well, to each his own," the young man said. "My name is Richard King. My uncle and I comprise the firm now that Mr. Huestiss is dead."

"So your clerk told me," she said.

His tone became businesslike. "Now what about your brother?"

She said, "His name is John Foster. I call him Johnny. Most people do. He is about your age. Perhaps you have met him."

"I don't think so," Richard King said. "I live a fairly quiet life. And I imagine you and your brother have only recently arrived in this country."

"Not too long ago," she agreed.

"The name is not familiar to me," the young lawyer said. "But do please go on."

She hesitated. Then she said, "Have you heard of the Contessa Maria Fillipio?"

A smile showed on his pleasant, boyish

face. "I'm not all that out of touch with things. Most of the papers mention her in their columns from time to time. She is supposed to be a great beauty and have many male admirers, isn't that so?"

"Yes," she agreed. She was thankful that he at least knew something of the Contessa. She went on, "Since you have read of her you must realize she has a somewhat tainted reputation."

"The papers didn't spell that out," he said. "But the tone of the stories did suggest that."

"She has been associated with the mysterious deaths of two prominent men," Adele said. "And I fear she has my brother marked for her next victim. And maybe myself as well. She has drawn Johnny into her circle and he has become a completely changed person."

Richard King listened with mild surprise. "Please give me all the details."

"I will try," she said, feeling more uneasy than before. She recited the events leading up to Johnny's ensnarement by the Contessa, trying to get everything in. When she came to the part where it was rumored that the woman might be a vampire she felt her cheeks burn. And when she finished there was a short silence in the barren office broken only by the raindrops on the window.

Richard King's young face was solemn. He rose from his chair and began to pace up and down in front of her. He said, "A most extraordinary story! I don't know what to make of it!"

"I need someone to help me," she pleaded. "My brother will pay no attention to my warnings."

"This woman must be a sinister person," the young lawyer said as he continued to pace up and down. "This Major must also be evil. They are apparently intent on trapping your brother and making him their victim."

"That is the way I see it," she said.

"I will not say that I can credit this talk of her being a vampire," the young lawyer went on. "But I surely can see that she is a scheming, dangerous woman. Perhaps even a murderess or at the very least an accessory to murder."

"So?"

Still pacing, Richard King went on as if talking to himself, "The thing is that we must try to apprehend these criminals before the deed is committed. That makes it very difficult."

"But surely their earlier crimes may be

proven against them. That would open the eyes of my brother, I would trust," she said.

The young lawyer halted and gazed at her with a frown on his round face. "That would be the ideal solution. But again it cannot be an easy one. As you know they have covered up any part in these earlier crimes very neatly. I think it might be almost impossible to link them with the two deaths you have mentioned in a criminal way."

She stared up at him in dismay. "You are saying my plight is hopeless?"

"No," he said. "I'm merely pointing out that this is going to be difficult."

"Money is no object," she said.

He, smiled at her indulgently. "I'm certain of that, and you must not think I'm attempting to frighten you into paying me a large retaining fee. That isn't my idea at all."

She blushed again. "I hadn't thought that. From the moment of our meeting I have felt that you could be my friend."

"I will try to be," Richard King said with sincerity. "The way I see it this isn't a task for a law firm at all."

"Then who?"

"Someone in the private investigation line," he told her. "And may I warn you at this point that many of them are not to be trusted? Too often they are renegades from police work using their training to cheat the unwary."

"Are there nothing but rogues in London?" she asked wearily.

"Sometimes it seems that is the case," he told her. "But I think there is one man who may be able to help you. The thing will be to interest him in your problem."

"Do you know him?"

"Fairly well," Richard King said. "He is a lawyer and used to have an office in this very building. But he has been retired from active practice of law for several years."

"Then he is elderly," she said in a disappointed tone.

"No," the young lawyer standing before her said. "As a matter of fact he is only in his late thirties and very active."

She was surprised. "Then why did he retire?"

"That is something else again," Richard King said turning mysterious in manner. "Would you be willing to place yourself in his hands?"

"Yes. Why not?"

"I must warn you that he is somewhat unorthodox as a person and in his manner of operations. He is not above enlisting figures from the underworld in his behalf if it helps him in his work."

"I see," she said.

The young lawyer gave her a knowing look. "That is why he no longer has a regular law practice. He finds he is often only able to bring his clients justice outside the courts, and often by means outside the law. Yet he is otherwise a completely honest man."

She stared up at him. "He must be a very complex person."

"He is. And let me say he is not interested in fees. If he takes on a case he does not wish payment in return. He has more money than he will ever need. He always requests that his fees be paid over to a home for foundlings which is a favorite charity of his. He once heard of the suicide of a lad whom Dr. Barnardo was forced to turn away from his home for lack of funds. And he has had a dedicated interest in the home since then."

"I would be glad to donate any sum he requests if he will only help my brother," she said.

Richard King nodded. "The great thing is to convince him that your brother is worth saving. Or from another viewpoint, to make him believe that the Contessa Maria is so dangerous to society that she must be checked."

"I'm sure she is monstrously wicked!" Adele exclaimed. "I cannot say she is a vampire. I do not know enough about such things. But something which happened to me last night made me wonder." And she told him about the bat which had entered her room.

He listened with great interest. "I agree that it does not seem possible it was a bat. I can go along with your brother's skepticism in that. But if you are right then I would say the creature must have been of supernatural origin. This is something which might interest my friend."

"Will you arrange for me to see him?"

He nodded. "Yes. I think it might be best for me to take you to him. He rarely sees people without their being introduced by someone whom he knows well. He has become a recluse."

"Indeed," she said, wondering what sort of man this might be.

"He lives in a cottage in a quiet lane on the outskirts of the city. Just he and a mute servant live in this house in Fetter Lane. The servant is a former seafaring man who had his tongue cut out in a brutal waterfront battle out East. He is admirable for my friend's purpose as there is no possibility of his gossiping."

"Then your friend is not married?" she said.

An odd look crossed the young lawyer's face, as he told her, "He was. He isn't anymore."

"May I ask his name?"

"Yes," Richard King said. "His name is Jeremy Quentain and I consider him the most courageous man I know."

"Jeremy Quentain," she said, repeating the name. "I like the ring of it if that is any omen."

The young lawyer smiled, "And if I can get him to see you I guarantee you will like the man."

"Could you take me to him right away?" Adele asked.

Richard King sat down in the swivel chair by his desk. He pulled out his gold pocket watch from his vest and consulted it. "It is almost lunch time now," he said. "I would not advise that we go there until early afternoon."

"I can come back," she suggested.

"Better than that," he said. "Why don't you take lunch with me? There are several fine restaurants not too far away. And while we are having the meal I can tell you more about Jeremy Quentain."

"There is more to know?"

"I have told you none of the important

things about him," the young lawyer said. "And I believe it is imperative that you know certain details before you meet him. It will enable you to put your full trust in him and understand him better."

She smiled ruefully. "I'm willing to take your word for his ability and character."

"Thank you," Richard King said. "But there are still facts which I wish to impart. We could leave for lunch now and then go directly from the restaurant to my friend's cottage in Fetter Lane."

She hesitated. "I do not wish to impose on you."

He smiled. "It would be a pleasure. Not too often do I have the company of attractive young ladies at luncheon."

She again realized how much she liked him and how he had impressed her from the moment she set eyes on him. It seemed stupid to be rigidly conventional and refuse to accompany him to the restaurant.

"Very well," she said with a smile. "I will accept your offer."

"Excellent," he said, jumping up. "My uncle is the famous member of the firm. I'm relatively unimportant so I can take time off when I like. I do my share of dull civil and estate work but I can work at that at my own pleasure."

"That is fortunate," she said, understanding that he was explaining why he was able to give her this time.

He went out and spoke to the clerk and then returned for her. He said, "I'm sure we'll have no trouble getting a cab. At this time of day they are up and down the street continually."

They went out together and waited in the doorway until he was able to hail a passing empty cab. He helped her up into it and as she sat down she happened to glance out the window and saw something which made her gasp aloud.

Richard King had just finished instructing the driver as to the location of the restaurant. He turned to her with some surprise to ask, "What is the matter?"

She indicated the window. "Over there. Lurking in that doorway! The man I know as Major Merrithew! He's in league with the Contessa! I'm afraid I was followed to your office!"

Chapter Three

Richard King turned on the seat and peered out through the small window at the rear of the cab. His pleasant face took on a surprised expression as he exclaimed, "By George, you're right! The fellow is running out into the street now and hailing a cab. He intends following us!"

"What can we do?" she worried.

"We're going to the Cafe Royal," the young lawyer told her. "It is in a fairly congested area. I'll have the driver stop short of it and we'll go there by some private ways I know of."

"I'm afraid of that man," she confessed. "It was he who lured my brother to that awful tavern on the docks."

"Just let me handle it," Richard King said. He opened the slit at the front of the cab and caught the driver's attention as he offered him new instructions.

She sat back in the shadowed interior of the jolting vehicle feeling dismayed. "Why should he want to follow me?" she wondered.

"They apparently have some plans for you as well as your brother," the lawyer told her. He glanced out the rear window again and said, "He's following us, all right. That's the cab with the same thin gray horse."

"He calls himself Major Merrithew," she said. "But I have doubts that he was ever in the army. He is nearly always drunk."

"A bad companion for your brother."

"The worst, since Johnny is ready enough to drink on his own," she said.

They journeyed to the busy center of the city and then the cab drew over to the curb and Richard King at once thrust a coin into the hand of the driver and hastily helped her to the crowded sidewalk.

Taking her by the arm he guided her along. Glancing back he murmured, "He's seen us get out and now he's leaving his cab as well. We'll have to move fast."

"Where are we going?" she asked.

"Just around the corner," the young lawyer said as they literally pushed their way along the crowded street, jostling some of the more sedate pedestrians.

As they turned the corner he quickly directed her into an arcade with an arched entrance. There were many small shops on either side of the arcade which was not as crowded as the street. He hurried her through it and out onto another street. Then they walked a block further to the entrance of the Cafe Royal.

She gave him a troubled look. "Do you think we've lost him?"

"I'm certain of it," Richard King said with a reassuring smile.

They entered the restaurant and were greeted by the headwaiter. Richard requested a quiet table and they were shown to one in a secluded corner at the back of the room.

After they were seated Richard told her, "This is ideal. Even if he does follow us here we'll be able to see him as soon as he enters. And I doubt that he would notice us away back here."

"I'm shocked that he should turn up that way," she said.

"You oughtn't to be," Richard King said. "No question you've warned your brother that you were going to seek outside help. He has undoubtedly let this drop in the presence of the Major. As they want to protect themselves they've decided to keep a close watch on you."

She gave the young lawyer a solemn look across the table. "I'm sure they mean to murder me along with my brother."

"I fear that is all too likely," Richard

King said with a sigh. "But maybe that will help us."

"Help us?" she said in a surprised voice.

He nodded. "The fact that your life is in danger is most likely to influence Jeremy Quentain in taking on your case. It is our ace card."

"Oh," she said.

"I'll explain more of that later," he said mysteriously. "But first let us order."

The menu of the Cafe Royal was as grand as the premises. The big restaurant quickly filled and there was a constant hum of conversation on the part of the fashionably-dressed men and their ladies. The aroma of good cigars was thick in the air and in the background a trio of musicians played. It reminded her of the fine restaurants in New York.

"This is much like Luchow's in New York," she told Richard King.

"It is perhaps my favorite restaurant," he told her. "Dickens patronized the place a good deal."

She was thrilled to hear this. "I have always enjoyed Dickens' novels."

The luncheon was served and proved to be a delicious roast of venison along with other interesting specialties of the fine restaurant. It was not until they had completed the lavish meal and were lingering over their coffee that they began to talk again.

The young lawyer said, "Evidently we lost the Major. He has not come in here."

"I feel so relieved," she said.

"You must expect more of the same," he warned her. "He is sure to follow you again."

"I suppose so," she sighed. "But perhaps by that time I may be under the protection of your Jeremy Quentain. Does he have agents whom he can assign to keep a protective watch on me?"

"I can't tell you too much about his methods," Richard was ready to admit. "But I do know that his servant, Ben, sometimes carries out errands for him. And I suspect when the occasion warrants it he recruits helpers from the underworld."

"Why not the police?"

"The police don't always approve of his methods."

"So he gets his henchmen from the other side of the law?"

"Yes. Jeremy is known in the underworld. He is feared and respected by most of the denizens of the criminal domain. Often he drops out of sight and spends weeks mingling with them."

She wrinkled her brow in speculation

about this. "He must be a most unusual person."

"He is. I think that now I must quickly tell you the rest about him before I try and get you an audience with him."

"Please do," she begged him. "For a start what does he look like?"

Richard smiled. "Trust a woman to want to know that."

"I don't mean it as a frivolous question," she protested. "I have the opinion that looks often tell us things about a person."

"I agree," he said. "Jeremy is about thirty, as I mentioned to you earlier. He is very spare of figure, and his face is also thin and highly intelligent. His nose is somewhat prominent and his eyes are burning under heavy dark brows. His mouth is thin and sensitive. All in all, his face is generally judged handsome by most people. I would dub him a handsome intellectual. He does not smile often and he usually dresses in dark or drab suits. His hair is jet black and romantically wavy. Think of an ascetic Byron and you have him."

"He sounds interesting. Was he a successful lawyer?"

"He was perhaps the most successful barrister in London. His prosecution of a number of criminal cases earned him a fine reputation. It also earned him the hatred of the underworld. He was especially a thorn in the side of an international crime organization headed by a mysterious figure called the Scorpion."

"That sounds like some sort of melodrama," she said.

"It is highly melodramatic," he agreed. "But alas, it is all true. This criminal known as the Scorpion warned Jeremy not to prosecute a case against one of the murderers in his employ. Jeremy paid no heed to the warning. As a result his lovely young wife was attacked and cruelly murdered while strolling in the nearby park one afternoon."

"How awful for him!" she gasped.

"It changed his life. For months he was a broken man unable to do anything. His grief was terrible to witness. Then after a time a gradual change came over him. He returned to his office and proceeded to wind up his affairs. It was whispered in legal circles that he had taken to opium to comfort him in his sorrow and that was why he was dropping out of the world he had so long dominated."

"Do you think this rumor was true?"

The young lawyer frowned. "I can't be certain. He may take drugs or he may not. One thing is positive, he does not indulge in any sort of drug when he is helping anyone.

It was after he gave up his office in the city and retired to the seclusion of his cottage that he began taking on cases of those oppressed or threatened by the criminal world. He turned from prosecution of criminals in the courts to fighting against them on the outside."

"And how has it turned out?"

"He has done a great deal of good. He has seen justice done where it seemed impossible that it could be done. And gradually a stratum of the underworld came to admire him and agree to help him. And if they refused he had just to threaten them with the kind of punishment only he is able to mete out."

"He sounds a very strong person."

"His grief in the loss of his wife has given him a steely strength and determination. Now people continually come to him for aid and he often sees that they get it."

"And you think he will have pity for me?"

"I'm almost certain he will," Richard King said. "He is still hoping to one day discover the identity of the Scorpion and settle with him for murdering his wife. This Contessa sounds as if she is the sort of criminal Jeremy Quentain particularly dislikes."

Adele sighed. "I can hardly wait to meet him."

"I trust that will happen shortly."

By the time they left the restaurant the downpour of rain had ended. They had no difficulty hailing a cab and were soon on their way to the cottage in which Jeremy Quentain lived. It was almost thirty minutes later when the cab drew up before a cottage of picture-book appearance set back from the street on quiet, pleasant Fetter Lane. There were a half-dozen other attractive houses on the cul-de-sac to give it a friendly look.

Richard King told her, "I will ask you to remain in the carriage until I learn whether Jeremy is at home and if he can see you."

"Very well," she said.

The young man's pleasant face showed sympathy. "I will be no longer than I can help. We'll keep the carriage for the return journey to the city in any case."

So he shut the carriage door and left her there to wait. She watched from the window and saw him walk up the flagstone path to the cottage and knock on the door. A moment later it was opened by a big, burly man of middle age. Richard King said something to the man and was at once shown inside. The door closed and she had nothing to do but sit back in the shadowed interior of the cab and wait.

She thought of all the things Richard King had told her about Jeremy Quentain and hoped the former lawyer would take on her problem. From the account given of him it struck her that he must be a lonely, unhappy man and that he'd taken to helping the oppressed to try and cure his unhappiness.

Johnny still worried her a great deal. She could not handle him any longer. She knew that if he were to be rescued from the clutches of the Contessa and her dissolute company help would be required. And from what Richard King had said, this Jeremy Quentain was the ideal man for the task.

The door of the cottage opened and Richard King came out quickly and made his way along the flagstone walk to the carriage. As he drew near she saw that he had a satisfied expression on his young face.

Opening the carriage door, he said, "We're in luck. Jeremy is at home and he will see you!"

She could not help being excited. "Did you explain my problem?"

"Briefly," he said. "I'm sure he'll want to ask you other questions." And he helped her down from the carriage and they strolled towards the door of the cottage together.

Now her nerves really became taut since

this was an important moment for her. Because she was so tense she found it difficult to carry on a casual conversation with the young lawyer. All she could think about was her confrontation with the legendary Jeremy Quentain.

Richard knocked on the door again and it was opened to them almost at once by the bald man with the surly face. He gave her a sharp glance and then stood back to let them enter a somewhat shadowed entrance hall. It was a modest hall and there was a door to the left which led to the drawing room. Richard King escorted her into the room and she saw the thin, male figure standing before the fireplace.

His back was to her as she entered and her first impression was of his slightly stooped shoulders and tall, spare build. He turned almost at once and she saw the handsome, intelligent face which Richard King had so aptly described. The alert, burning eyes in the narrow sensitive face fixed on her and he held out a thin hand to her.

"My dear Miss Foster," he said.

"Thank you for seeing me, Mr. Quentain," she told him in a voice with a slight tremor in it.

"Richard has told me about your problem," the tall man in the dark suit said, still studying her closely as he spoke. "Be good enough to have a chair."

"Thank you!" She sat in the chair nearest her and gazed up at the former lawyer.

His handsome, melancholy face showed a slight frown. "Your great concern is this Contessa Maria Fillipio and what she is doing to your brother."

"Yes," she said. Richard stood quietly behind her chair and said nothing. It was evident that he wanted the exchange to be completely between her and the man in black.

Jeremy Quentain said, "You believe they mean to lead your brother to his death and take your life as well?"

"I'm convinced they are after our fortune," she said. "And I know of two others who died under mysterious circumstances and who left the whole of their estates to this evil woman."

The tall, handsome man nodded. "I know of the cases as well. I have not been unaware of the Contessa's machinations. I find it a strange coincidence that you should come to me at a time when I have been considering what to do about her."

Adele had been so taken by the magnetic quality of his personality that she had forgotten for a moment that she had come there to plead for his help. Now his words brought this back to her and gave her encouragement that she wouldn't be turned away.

She said, "You will help me then?"

"Yes," Jeremy Quentain said in his deep, pleasant voice. "You can count on my aid. You know this will be a dangerous business. Your brother has mixed himself up in a hornet's nest of trouble."

"I realize that," she said.

The tall man went on, "I have reason to believe the Contessa is only a tool in the hands of an even more dangerous archcriminal with whom I have a personal score to settle."

Richard King stepped forward and spoke for the first time in a shocked tone. "You mean she is allied with the Scorpion?"

"If my information is correct," Jeremy Quentain said gravely. "And I may say that it usually is."

Hesitantly, Adele asked him, "Have you heard the other thing? That she may have supernatural powers."

Jeremy Quentain eyed her directly. "You're referring to the rumors that she may be a vampire."

"Yes," she said.

"I have heard about that," he agreed.

"And I think there may be truth in it. I understand the Scorpion has lately turned to the use of the living dead to carry out his vicious schemes. Vampires are controllable and ask little in return for their services."

"They ask the blood of innocents," Richard King said. "Do you think that little?"

Jeremy Quentain gave him a grim smile. "I do not, but I fear that this is the opinion of the Scorpion."

Adele asked, "How will you go about helping me?"

"I shall begin by making some discreet enquiries," Jeremy said. "You must not be impatient. You may think nothing is happening. I assure you I shall be at work on your behalf from this moment."

"What about my brother?" she worried.

"I shall try to warn him," the man in black said. "And if he does not respond I shall attempt to prove to him that he is putting himself and you in great danger."

"When will I hear from you again?" she asked.

"I shall contact you when I have some progress to report," Jeremy Quentain said.

Richard King spoke up. "What if Adele is faced with some special threat in the meantime?"

"Then she may contact me," Jeremy replied. "I heard about your narrow escape from those thugs last night," he said, turning to her again. "The weapons they used are common in the underworld. I know most of these types and how they operate. The palmers, shofulmen and snakesmen have few secrets from me!"

"Those are names I've never heard before," she confessed.

He offered her another of his grim smiles, "I was referring to shoplifters, passers of bad money, and boy thieves employed in housebreaking, using the terms of the underworld."

Richard King gave her a knowing glance. "Jeremy not only understands these people but he can talk on their level."

"I find that useful," Jeremy said. "Now there will be a fish peddler with a barrow along your street several times a day from now on. His name is Alfie and he is a squat little man with a loud, hoarse voice cultivated in selling his wares. He is an agent of mine. Should you wish to consult me give your message to him. He will inform me quickly."

She listened to this with some awe. "You are going to install this man in the area of our house for my protection?"

"Exactly," Jeremy Quentain said. "He will keep an eye open for suspicious characters such as this Major Merrithew of whom Richard has told me. And he will be close by to give you physical aid should you need it."

"You are more thorough than I guessed," she marveled.

He said, "Alfie will not be my only agent engaged in your behalf. But for the success of our venture I prefer to keep the names and identities of the others secret for the moment."

"You are most kind," she said. "I do not know how to thank you."

"I do not expect thanks," he told her. "I believe you heard me say that my information suggested the Scorpion is the master mind behind the Contessa's operations. This makes it something of a personal feud for me."

"I understand," she said sympathetically.

"The fight against evil operates on a broad field. But very often one evil is linked with another. So it is in this case."

"This is such a macabre business," Adele said with a shudder. "It is difficult to know how to battle an enemy who may be one of the living dead."

"You must be extremely cautious," Jeremy Quentain said. "Do not expose yourself to any dangers you do not understand. I think you may have had a close call when that bat entered your room. Are you wearing the crucifix?"

"Yes," she said.

"Keep it with you always," was the tall man's advice. "I will be in touch with you as soon as I can. In the meanwhile know that you are not alone in this."

Adele got to her feet. "I shall be forever grateful to you if you can save my brother."

"I will do my best," Jeremy Quentain promised her.

Then he saw them to the door and on their way. When they were in the carriage and headed back to London she turned to the young lawyer at her side and asked, "Do you think Mr. Quentain is truly interested in my plight?"

"He is not a man to talk without meaning it," Richard told her. "I'm sure he is going to help you."

"I find him very strange," she said. "So aloof. All the while he was talking to us it was as if he were thinking of something else."

"He has a preoccupied manner," the young lawyer agreed. "But do not be put off by it."

"I liked him," she was quick to add. "But

he is very different. There is such an air of sadness about him."

"That has been so only since the murder of his wife," the man beside her said. "But he was always a person of reserve."

The journey back to the city seemed to take less time than the journey out to Fetter Lane. Richard saw her to her door and doffed his top hat as he bade her goodbye.

"I hope we may meet soon again," he said.

She gave him a grateful smile. "I have troubled you enough as it is."

"There was no trouble involved," Richard King said with sincerity. "I have enjoyed meeting you and I trust that I may see you again. Have I your permission to call?"

Blushing, she said, "Of course, if you like. But I warn you that my brother's safety comes first. I may be deeply involved in trying to help him for the next several weeks."

"Perhaps I may be able to help," Richard King suggested. "I do not mean as a lawyer but in a personal way. We cannot let Jeremy Quentain take on all the burden."

"That is kind of you," she said, studying his pleasant face and thinking that she liked him a great deal.

"Very well then," he said. "You shall hear from me and soon. I would much like us to have another meal together. Until then, all my good wishes."

She thanked him and went inside feeling happier than she had in a long while. Not only had she accomplished something in trying to aid her errant brother, she had in the process of doing this made a good friend. And at the moment she had few such friends in London. She felt it might be the beginning of happier days for her. But this did not turn out to be the case.

She met Marlow in the hallway and asked him, "Has my brother returned?"

"No, Miss," the old man said with a troubled look on his wizened face.

"Let me know if he does."

"Yes, Miss."

She went upstairs and rested for a little. Then she changed for dinner. But when she went downstairs she found that Johnny had still not returned and she was faced with having dinner alone.

It was a cheerless meal. She ate hardly anything and all the time she worried about her brother. When she left the dining room she came upon Marlow as he descended the broad stairway into the hall. The old hunchback had a worried look.

He came down to her and confided, "I have just spoken with Mr. Johnny's valet and he tells me that he packed a bag for him when he left this morning. He assumed that Mr. Johnny was going off on some sort of journey."

She felt a surge of fear. "He certainly didn't mention any journey to me," she said.

"I thought you ought to know, Miss," Marlow said.

"He packed enough clothing to assume my brother was making some journey?"

"Yes."

She frowned. "What can it mean?"

"I asked if he mentioned when he would be back and his valet claims that he made no comment about this," the old servant said.

Adele was stunned. "I don't understand."

"Is there anything I can do?" the old man asked.

She shook her head. "I can't think of anything just now. I'll let you know."

The news had shaken her. She went into the big drawing room with its crystal chandelier lighted with gas and began to pace up and down. She felt this was enough of a crisis to get in touch with Jeremy Quentain but it was too early to contact him. He had told her his agent would be in the area posing as a peddler in the morning. Tonight there was no one she could turn to.

In her desperation and concern about

Johnny she made an impulsive decision. She would go to the house of the Contessa and confront her. She would demand to know where Johnny had gone. It might be that the Contessa had left on a trip somewhere and taken Johnny with her. In any event it seemed likely that going to the Contessa's house would bring her closer to the truth.

She went out and found Marlow and asked him, "Please have the carriage ready for me."

"Yes, Miss," the old man said. "I have been talking to the coachman. And he told me that he took Mr. Johnny to the house of the Contessa this morning."

Her lovely face was grim. "That doesn't surprise me, Marlow. I suspected it. Well, he can take me there now."

The ancient hunchback showed surprise and concern. "You are going to that woman's house?"

"Why not?" she said. "I can't let her know that I fear her. And I can't postpone trying to find out what my brother is going to do."

"Do you wish me to go with you?" Marlow asked.

"No," she said. "The coachman will be enough. I will have him wait for me."

The old man licked his thin lips nervously. "I don't like it at all, Miss."

77

"You mustn't worry," she told him. "I'm sure I'll be all right."

She went upstairs to put on her cloak while he summoned the carriage. A tinge of uneasiness bothered her. She knew that Jeremy Quentain had warned her to be careful and not to attempt too much on her own. But she needed to know what had happened to Johnny at once. By morning he could be murdered and she couldn't contact Jeremy Quentain until then. The former lawyer had not seen the need for her getting in touch with him before then but now she was faced with a crisis!

She thought of Richard King and knew he would gladly help her. But she had not found out his home address and he would not be in his office at this evening hour. She had no alternative but to seek out the Contessa on her own. As she put on her cloak she felt inside her bodice and was comforted by the feel of the crucifix chain still there.

Marlow had the carriage waiting for her when she went downstairs. The ancient servant again pleaded with her to allow him to accompany her but she refused. She could not see that he would be of any use. The coachman would be along. She told the coachman where she wanted to go and he admitted to knowing the address well.

"I often take Mr. Johnny there," the coachman said.

"And you last took him there this morning?"

"Yes."

"He had a large suitcase with him, I understand?"

"That is so, Miss," the coachman agreed.

He helped her into the carriage and then drove her to the Contessa's house. The street on which the house was located was narrow and dark. The sight of it caused Adele some alarm, but she could not turn back at this point.

The coachman glanced up at the house as he assisted her to the sidewalk. "This is it, Miss. You wish me to wait?"

"I do," she agreed. "I don't expect to be long. If I'm in there more than fifteen minutes will you please come in for me?"

The coachman's broad face showed surprise but he said, "Very well, Miss."

She gazed up at the house and saw that there were no lights on the ground floor. Indeed the windows on that floor were shuttered. But high above, on the third floor, a pale yellow glow of light showed through several of the windows. It was a grim, menacing house and again she felt a growing sense of fear. But she fought her terror and mounted the several steps to the front door. There was an outside door which gave access to a vestibule and an inner door. She tried the outside door and it opened easily.

With a pounding heart she ventured into the darkness of the vestibule, and just as she did so, a clawlike hand sprang out of the shadows and grasped her arm!

Chapter Four

Adele drew back and screamed with fear! The grip on her arm was not lessened. At the same time an ugly face appeared out of the shadows of the vestibule and thrust itself close to hers. The features were grotesque like those of some cross between a human and a parrot and criss-crossed with wrinkles. Mad eyes glittered at her from the old woman's ruined face as the crone uttered a high-pitched cackle almost as loud as Adele's scream.

"Don't be afraid, Missy! Old Meg won't hurt you! All I need is a tuppence for a bit of gin!" the toothless hag babbled at her.

The stench of the repulsive old woman almost made her ill, not to mention the shock of being assaulted in this fashion by her. She tried to free herself from the crone's viselike grip with no success.

"Please let me go!" she begged the ancient one.

The high-pitched cackle came again from the sunken mouth of old Meg. "Won't you

81

give me tuppence, luv? It's not much for the likes of you!"

Adele did not know what to do but her predicament was swiftly solved as the inner door opened and a tall, white-haired man with a stern face and a gray beard appeared. The glow from a hall lamp inside now illuminated the vestibule.

The bearded man at once gave his attention to the old crone in her loathesome rags. "I have driven you away from here before," he cried angrily. "How dare you come back? I'll have the police on you!"

Old Meg let go her hold on Adele's arm and at once became a cringing beggar before the authority of the bearded one. "Don't do that, good sir! I'll leave! I'll never come back! I promise!"

"Scum!" the heavy-set bearded man said with disgust.

Old Meg took this as a cue to vanish. She quickly turned and hurled open the outer door and ran into the street. Left alone to face the gray-bearded one Adele felt herself trembling.

Now the graybeard addressed himself to her, saying, "And what are you doing here at this time of night, Miss Foster?"

"You know me?" she said, astonished.

His heavy-featured face showed a sarcastic smile. "It is my business to know people, Miss Foster. I am the Contessa's manager and protector."

"You are Carlos," she said. "My brother has spoken of you."

"Indeed?" the man said mockingly. "But you have not answered my question. Why have you come here?"

"I'm looking for my brother."

"What makes you think he's here?"

"I'm sure he must be," she said.

Carlos looked crafty. "How can I convince you that you are wrong?"

"I'm afraid you can't," she said. "He left our home early today with a packed suitcase. As if he were embarking on some journey. I'm sure the Contessa knows about it."

"You are wrong!"

"I think not," she said. "And I demand to see the Contessa and be allowed to talk with her."

"So that is what you want," Carlos said. "You must know the Contessa Maria Fillipio is a woman of high position. She does not deign to see everyone who comes uninvited to her door!"

Adele paid no attention to his words. She was not going to be put off so easily. She said, "I demand to see the Contessa!"

"Even though she knows nothing about your brother?"

"I don't believe that!"

The man called Carlos laughed softly. "It seems the Contessa must give you an audience."

"Unless she does I'm going to the police," Adele threatened emptily, knowing the police would pay no attention to such a complaint.

"That would be wasted time on your part," the man with the gray beard and thick gray hair said. "But no need to discuss this. I am quite willing to take you up to the Contessa."

"Then let us waste no more time," she said.

"Come along, Miss Foster," Carlos said in his mocking way. He drew back for her to enter the musty hallway. And then he led her up the long, shadowed stairway.

She marched up the stairs beside him, terrified by the weird atmosphere of the old mansion. It was more like a deserted house than one being lived in by a notorious woman-about-town. The wallpaper looked damp and was peeling in places and the painted woodwork was worn and shabby. She could not imagine why her brother was attracted to such people and such a place.

They climbed a second flight of stairs to the third floor from which she'd seen lights at the windows. They came to giant double doors at the rear of the landing and Carlos halted and turned to her.

"I warn you the Contessa will not be pleased to see you. Do you still wish to impose yourself on her?"

"Yes," she said firmly, hiding the fact that her resolution was not nearly as strong as it had been.

"Very well, then," Carlos said with a kind of sneer. "It is on your own head!"

He drew the double doors open to reveal a high-ceilinged room decorated in a style of Oriental splendor. Rich drapes vied with thick Persian carpets and elegant furniture to create the atmosphere of wealth and love of the exotic. There was a lushness about the crimson-dominated room which suggested decadence.

Carlos smiled as he saw her reaction to the room. He said, "You are impressed? You should be. Not only is the Contessa a unique woman, she also has unique talents!"

She made no answer to this as she tried to pull herself together for whatever ordeal might lie ahead. She knew she had impulsively, and perhaps foolishly, gotten herself into this situation, and now she must be ready to pay for her lack of caution.

The room smelled of some sort of heady incense and the rich, baroque furniture was epitomized by a divan at the far side of the room decorated in glistening ruby satin and covered with cushions in lush yellows and greens. She guessed that it was from this divan that the Contessa would hold court.

Carlos crossed the room and vanished behind high gray drapes which hung the length of the wall behind the divan. The whole atmosphere of the place made her uneasy. She stood alone in the middle of the big room with its muted lighting from several huge white globes containing gas lamps. And once again she had the terrifying feeling she was being spied on by unseen eyes.

She began to feel faint and wasn't sure whether it was because of her fear or the heady incense whose aroma was drowning her nostrils. Then she saw the drapes part at the point where Carlos had vanished. And for a brief moment she had a distant view of the room beyond. What she saw made her hold her breath for a moment. For she was sure that in the back of the other room there stood an elaborate coffin!

Now a figure appeared in the opening between the drapes. It was the Contessa! The dark-haired woman was wearing a dress of great elegance which seemed to gleam under the lights, its gold threads catching their brightness. The bosom of the Contessa's gown was cut startlingly low, and much of her bare back was also revealed.

The Contessa glided forward rather than walked. She carried a fan of the same golden hue as her gown. It was her face which most caught Adele's attention. For the Contessa had a soft, feminine cast of features with large brown eyes, and jet black hair drawn back from her forehead. Her face was oval and she was strikingly beautiful. Yet there was an air of menace about her.

She gazed at Adele with upraised chin as she demanded, "How dare you intrude on me in this way?" Her voice had a husky pleasant quality with a hint of an accent.

"I have come about my brother," Adele said.

"Your brother?" Contessa Maria showed disdain. "Why should I know anything about your brother?"

"You do," she insisted.

"Your saying that does not make it so," the Contessa said languidly and she glided across to the satin divan and settled down on it to hold the fan to her bosom as she gazed at Adele in a cool and insolent manner.

Adele fought her nervousness to say, "My brother is in love with you. You can't deny that!"

The Contessa smiled in an amused fashion. "And what if he is, my girl? What do you expect to do about it? Surely not make him change his mind?"

"I want him free of you," she said desperately. "You have some sort of frightening hold on him! Please let him go! Send him home to me!"

"That is a very touching plea," the Contessa said, using her fan to cool herself in the warm, scented room.

"I hope it will reach your heart," Adele said, choked with emotion.

"It might well do that if I were causing some harm to your brother. I am not!"

"I have come here tonight to ask you to send him home with me," Adele said unhappily. "It is not easy for me to get down on my knees before someone I hate!"

The Contessa Maria Fillipio smiled in cold fashion. "How touching these little revelations of yourself are. But they ought not to be directed to me, but to Johnny himself."

"Then you admit he is here!"

"I admit nothing," the Contessa said, her voice hard once more.

Adele was all excitement. "May I see my brother? Please let me talk with him!"

The Contessa looked amused. "I might just decide to do that."

The drapes in the rear wall were parted again and the familiar face and figure of Major Merrithew came into view. The look of triumph on his bloated, purplish countenance as he glanced at Adele showed that he felt he had won over her. Now he went to the divan where the Contessa was resting and whispered something to her.

The Contessa smiled slightly and Adele was more than ever aware of the woman's thick red lips. There was a different look about the mouth of the Contessa — call it voluptuous, or even greedy. And as she thought about this she could not help debating whether the beautiful woman might be a vampire or not. It was said that vampires could be singled out by the telltale nature of their mouths.

The Contessa spoke again in her husky voice. "I have just received word that your brother is here."

"I'm sure he's been here all along," she said defiantly.

"Your opinion is of no interest to me," the Contessa said. "But since you wish to blame me for causing him to stray I think it might be best for you to see him and talk to him."

"You will let me?" She was surprised.

"Why not?" the Contessa asked. She turned to the Major. "I'm sure you've met the Major."

"I have."

"He shall be your escort to your brother. And I trust that when you have had a talk with him you will in no way blame me for what his state of mind may be."

"Take me to him," she said.

The Contessa turned to the waiting Major and said, "Very well, Major. Take her to see her brother. Remember, I will hold you responsible for her safety."

The Major nodded and then he walked over to Adele and said, "If you want to see Johnny, come with me."

"You know I want to see him!" she said annoyed.

"Follow me, then," the Major ordered her.

She had no choice but to do so. Inwardly she was very much afraid but she felt everything depended on her getting to see Johnny and having a talk with him. In her desperation she had decided to let her brother know she had sought professional help to separate him from his evil companions.

As she turned to follow the Major she saw

a sneering sort of smile on the Contessa Maria's face. The woman was obviously enjoying Adele's humbling herself. The Major led her down a dark hall and out the double doors. Then they walked a distance in near darkness before they reached a stairway.

"Watch your step," he told her. "These stairs are both narrow and steep. I don't want to deliver you to Johnny in an injured state."

At once she said, "Why won't you leave him alone?"

The man on the stairway ahead of her said, "I think your brother enjoys my company."

"You cause him to drink too much," she protested, carefully following after him.

He laughed harshly. "Johnny can out-drink me any day. You have a naive opinion of your brother. He is not the sort of man you think. I assure you of that."

They had reached the bottom of the stairway and she still could not tell where she was because of the darkness. She wondered that the Major could get around so easily without any sort of light but guessed that he knew the building well.

The Major turned to her and said, "I will guide you by taking your arm."

"How can you see in this darkness?" she wondered aloud.

"It is not as difficult as you might think," he told her, taking her arm. There was a grim note of amusement in his words which baffled her.

She said, "How long have you been a friend of the Contessa?"

"A long while," he said.

"Does Johnny really love her?"

The Major said, "I was instructed to take you to your brother, not to answer all your questions. I fear you will have to find out some of these things by yourself."

"I will," she promised.

"Let me tell you one thing," the Major said in his hoarse drinker's voice. "You will never be a match for the Contessa. In any battle of wits with her you are bound to lose."

"Thank you for being so frank," she told him. "But you haven't frightened me at all."

"Here we are," the Major said, pausing at a point in a pitch-black corridor.

She gazed ahead of her worriedly and asked him, "Why would my brother be in a place like this?"

"He is not in the darkness," the Major said. "Only the passages are grim in this old house. The rooms off them are quite lavish as you must have noticed when you were upstairs."

"Where is my brother?" she demanded, growing more suspicious and afraid every moment. She began to fear she had fallen into some trap. She could not believe that Johnny was waiting anywhere here in this dark, neglected portion of the old house.

The Major reached out in the blackness and swung open a door which gave entry to another dark room. His hand still on her arm, he told her, "In there!"

She held back. "There's no one in there!"

"You're wrong!" was the reply in his hoarse, menacing voice and he roughly shoved her into the room and closed the door on her.

It happened so swiftly she hadn't even time to make a protest or try and escape from the iron grip he'd had on her. But once she was abandoned in the room she began to pound on the door and sob out for him not to leave her there. His only reply was to turn a key in the lock and walk away.

She heard his retreating footsteps with despair. After trying the door again she turned around to see what sort of place she was in. There was a small break in the utter darkness and she strained her eyes to discover that it marked a window in the opposite wall of the room.

Encouraged, she rushed across to the window. But when she reached it she found it was barred. She grasped the two bars which were firmly in place and tried to see out. She could merely get a glimpse of a blank brick wall opposite. The night outside was just a trifle lighter than the blackness of the room, that was her only comfort.

Now she turned to try and see something of the room once again. It seemed to be empty of any furniture, which did not surprise her. And it had evidently been fitted out as a kind of prison cell. The Contessa had tricked her into being made a prisoner. What would the malevolent woman do next? What had she in mind for her?

The room was damp and filled with the stench of decay. Now panic began to well up in her. And she realized that she had been completely foolish in allowing her impatience to get her into such a trap. She had been mad to make the excursion to see the Contessa on her own! She should have obeyed Jeremy Quentain and waited for him to tell her what to do!

Now she was likely never to be heard of again. And Johnny was too much under the influence of the evil woman to take much notice. They would keep him drunk for days and when he had given over his estate to them in his will they would see that he met his death in the same fashion as those other two victims.

She groped her way across the shadows of the room to the door again and pounded on it and called out for help. But she might just as well have saved her efforts. There was no reply. She was in some deserted section of the old building where she could not be heard. Her captors had taken good care of this.

If her brother were in the house he'd probably be upstairs somewhere in the apartment of the Contessa. Memory of that scented, satin-decorated place brought back another memory. A more shocking one! Memory of that coffin she had glimpsed briefly in the corner of the Contessa's bedroom!

It surely meant that the gossip was right! That the Contessa was indeed a vampire! But she would have little chance of proving this. Little chance of doing anything now that she'd allowed herself to be made a prisoner. The Contessa would see that her lips were safely sealed in one way or another.

A rat scurried across the floor of the room

close by, making a complaining, squeaking sound. She cried out in fear and pressed tightly against the door. She had no idea how long they might attempt to keep her in this place and whether she could endure it long without collapsing.

It was bad enough to be a captive while she was aware of everything around her and could battle to protect herself. But what if she became unconscious? She had heard macabre stories of the vicious wounds made on helpless children by the huge dockside rats! And she had seen specimens of the cruel tribe when she'd visited the wharves; she had shuddered at their beady red eyes and the long, cruel teeth! What might such grim creatures do to her if she fell helpless to the floor of the dark room?

The thought was not comforting. A chill fear took over from the impatient panic she'd known when first imprisoned. Now she knew how desperate her position was and how little she could do about it. Jeremy Quentain had warned her and she had chosen not to heed his warning.

She gave her attention to the window again and clenched the bars and lifted herself up a little. As her eyes rose above the level of the sill she was able to get a brief look down into the street and saw the glow of a gas light down there. It filled her with a desperate longing to be free.

The grimy glass windows beyond the bars had some sort of fine mesh covering them. This protective wire made them impervious to being shattered. It would be useless to try and break one of the panes and shout her pleas for safety from there. She could only wait and hope that the fate planned for her by the wicked Contessa would not be too awful.

Yet knowing the woman and the nature of her reputation she could not believe there was any real hope. The best she could expect would be a quick death. That would be the most merciful but she doubted that the evil gang who'd captured her would be content with that.

What about the coachman? She had particularly instructed him to enter the old house in search of her if she did not return in fifteen minutes. The fifteen minutes were now long over. What had he done? Surely he would have made some effort to carry out her instructions!

And then she imagined a scene in which the Major would go down to the door and tell the coachman to leave. The wily Major would pretend to be offering a message from her and ask the coachman to drive back home. No doubt the Major assured him that she had decided to stay longer and would find other means to get back.

This rang so true she could almost hear the exchange between the two men. The Major would know she had come in her own carriage and would take care to see the coachman was dismissed in this manner. She could look for no help from that quarter.

Another rat scurried by squeaking and sent her into a fresh fit of horror. She could not bear the place! Again she pounded on the door until her fists ached and shouted until her voice was strained. Then she pressed weakly against it and sobbed quietly.

She was still sobbing when she first heard the scraping sound and worried about what new horror she might be in for. Then, as she listened, she was able to localize the sound. It was on the other side of the door. Actually it seemed that someone was working on the door lock itself.

Turning she watched with frightened eyes and then she heard the knob turn and the door was very gradually opened. She stepped back to be prepared for any attack. Whoever it was crept carefully into the room and whispered her name, "Miss Foster!"

She could not guess who it might be. But they knew her name. And in a taut voice, she replied, "Yes!"

"Miss Foster!" her name was repeated, and the voice seemed recognizable. She had heard it before.

"What is it?"

"Come quickly with me!" the phantom figure urged her.

Still not able to see who it was, she said, "All right." And she blindly followed the unknown one out into the corridor.

A hand touched her arm. "Make no sound and keep close to me," she was bidden.

"Who are you?" she whispered.

"Later," came the impatient reply in a whisper.

They hurried along the corridor and then down two flights of stairs. They reached a damp cellar and Adele felt the uneven ground under her feet. Then she was guided over to a short set of stairs which led upward. She mounted them with her rescuer and in a moment stepped out into the open.

She was standing in the blackness of an alleyway and at her side crouched the old beggar woman, Meg. The wrinkled face with the huge hooked nose, framed by the wild disarray of loose gray hair, held an anxious expression as the old woman peered about them.

"Come along!" old Meg said and fairly ran out the alley to the street.

She followed her without any questions. She could only be grateful for having been saved from that prison room. They kept moving until they came to a storefront and old Meg dodged into it and crouched in the shadows.

Joining her, Adele said, "Thank you so much!"

Old Meg shook her head. "We're not out of the woods yet!"

"How did you know they'd made me a prisoner?" she asked tautly.

The old woman looked grim. "You are a child!"

Then there was the sound of voices back where they had come from. Male voices in urgency: Adele recognized that they belonged to Carlos and the Major. The two were exchanging shouts and running down the street, coming directly towards them!

"Careful!" old Meg hissed and drew Adele close by her in the deep shadows of the doorway.

Adele watched and waited with bated breath. The two men came running by the doorway and didn't halt. They were clearly in search of her, having gone to the room and learned of her escape. Their racing footsteps and hoarse voices faded in the distance.

"Now!" old Meg snapped, and she grasped Adele by the arm and led her out of the doorway.

"Where?" she asked breathlessly.

"Leave that to me!" the old beggar woman told her. She ran with surprising rapidity for a woman of her age, crossing the street and dodging down a narrow alley, then through a passage so narrow they had to squeeze their way sideways. This brought them into another mean street. The old woman hurried on again until they came to a tavern.

The tavern was dimly lighted and there seemed to be a crowd inside from the noise which issued through its doors. Above it hung a faded sign, "The Gull and Herring."

"To the rear," old Meg ordered her and headed down the dark alley next to the tavern.

Adele was in no position to question her. She followed quickly until they reached the end of the alley. Then they halted breathlessly and the old crone pounded on a rear door there. From inside the sound of an accordion could be heard along with singing, laughter and the usual shouts of drunken revelry.

After what seemed an eternity the door was flung open and a stocky man with a kind of red nightcap on his head gazed out at them with an ugly look on his face. But when he saw Meg a light of recognition replaced his scowl.

"It's you, Meg!" he exclaimed.

"Who did you expect, the Queen?" old Meg retorted in disgust. "Let me and my friend in!"

The stocky man's coarse laughter rent the night air. He drew back. "Welcome, your Majesties!" he said mockingly. "Welcome to the Gull and Herring!"

Meg nimbly stepped up and entered the dimly lit back room. Adele followed her, wondering what it all meant. The stocky man shut and carefully bolted the door. Then he came back to them and it was only then that Adele noticed he had a wooden leg. A peg leg to be exact, its rod protruding from the bottom of his left pants leg.

The stocky man saw her staring at his leg and guffawed. His coarse face showed no annoyance as he said, "Left the real one in the Crimea, Miss! The damn Russkies took it from me!"

"Oh!" she said, not knowing how to answer.

Old Meg stood in the shadowed room and pulled her shawl around her. "Get me a gin, Bill," she ordered the man in the red nightcap tartly.

The stocky man leered at her. "Sure, Meg, long as you have the money to pay for it!"

"Don't worry about that!" the crone snapped, her parrot face all indignation.

"I won't," the stocky man said. "If you're short you've but to go on to the West End and sell your lovely body to a fine gent!" And then he guffawed at his own joke.

"Gin, you fool!" Meg said angrily.

"Sure, Meg," the stocky man said, cutting short his laughter. It was clear that he really had respect for her. Then he gave Adele a knowing look and said, "What can I get for you, pretty one?"

"You let her alone!" Meg ordered. "She's a lady!"

"Of course she is!" the stocky man mocked. "Any friend of old Meg's is bound to be a lady! What are you doing, Meg, teaching her the tricks of the trade?"

Meg looked as if she were ready to strike him with her scrawny old fist but the tension of the moment was relieved by a loud knocking on the rear door again. The stocky man looked uneasy and asked Meg, "That won't be the police, will it? They aren't after you?"

"Why should they be?" Meg asked defensively.

The coarse face of the stocky man showed anger. "I know what you're up to these days. Stick a knife in the ribs and off with a purse! Slash the leather of milady's pocketbook and run off with it! What was it tonight, Meg?"

"I'm not wanted! I swear it!" Meg told him.

"You'd better not be," he warned her, "or I'll turn you over."

Adele watched with frightened eyes as the stocky man went to the door. She fully expected that when he opened it Major Merrithew and Carlos would come rushing in to seize her.

But when the stocky man cautiously drew back the door a very different figure was revealed. A tall, spare man in tattered rags and wearing a shabby black top hat came groping his way up into the room. He had a cane in his hand and his eyes were covered by black glasses.

"Blimey!" the stocky one said in surprise. "It's Blind Paul!"

"So it is!" old Meg said, suddenly smiling. "Good evening to you, Blind Paul!"

"And to you, Meg," came the reply from the blind man. Only the voice was not that of a street vagrant but of a man of culture. Adele knew she had heard it before!

Chapter Five

Staring at the tall, blind beggar she suddenly exclaimed, "It's you!"

Blind Paul stood before her and removed his dark glasses and battered top hat and she saw revealed the handsome, ascetic face of Jeremy Quentain. The former lawyer had shaded his face with some sort of dark coloring to give it a different look but there was no mistaking him.

"You are quite correct, Miss Foster," he said in his own sonorous voice. "You can count yourself lucky that I was at hand tonight to help you. And that Meg took such a risk to get you out of that house."

She glanced from him to the old crone and saw the amused smile on the wrinkled face of the ancient Meg. She said, "You work with Mr. Quentain?"

Meg chuckled. "There are those who say so. Let us leave it at that — I do him a favor now and then. And I'd still like that gin, Bill!"

Bill nodded and turned to Jeremy

Quentain to ask, "What can I do for you, sir?"

"Sherry for the young lady and myself," the tall man said. "And I'll look after Meg's bill as well."

Bill's coarse face took on a crafty expression of amusement. "Right, sir! As long as you're paying she can have all the gin she likes!" And he went off to the front room of the pub to get the drinks.

Meg glanced after him with an expression of disgust on her aged, sunken face. "Publican clod!" she said. And she settled herself in a nearby plain chair.

Jeremy Quentain eyed Adele with a look of concern. "You have been through a most unpleasant experience. You must be exhausted."

"I am rather tired," she admitted.

"Do sit down," he said, waving to another chair near old Meg's. The tiny room behind the pub boasted only the two chairs, a stool, and a plain wooden table.

She sat and then said, "I know you must think me an idiot."

His thin face had a bland look. "I think you forgot my warnings. And I'd say you used very poor judgement."

"I know that now," she said. "But I was so upset at Johnny not coming home. I felt I

107

couldn't wait until morning and I had a desire to meet that awful woman and tell her what I thought of her."

Jeremy said, "I can understand your feelings but I deplore your giving in to them. You must know that is a house of danger."

Old Meg broke in. "If I wasn't handy in picking a lock you would still be a prisoner there, luv!"

"I know that and I'm grateful to you," she said.

The tall man standing before them said, "You can be grateful to her for more than that. She was watching the house when you went in and she reported your arrival to me. I sent her back to try and help you. Luckily she was able to. But that was only a fortunate circumstance. It could have been quite different for you. Quite tragic!"

"I didn't know what to do when they locked me in that dark, awful place," she said.

"Their plans for you wouldn't have ended there," Jeremy said with a grave expression on his handsome face. "I think the Contessa had something more in mind."

"I have no doubt of that," Adele said.

The ancient Meg nodded. "She is a wicked one!"

Bill came back carrying a tray with their

drinks. "Cheer for all!" he announced and he gave Adele her sherry first, then he handed Jeremy his, giving the gin to old Meg last. With a grin he told the old woman, "That will do your dry throat a bit of good!"

Meg sniffed. "I expect I'll have to make do with it," she told him. "Watered gin if I ever tasted any!"

Bill's good-natured look vanished. "Don't be saying such things, old woman! I run a first-class house!"

Jeremy spoke up. "I'm sure Meg agrees in that. She was merely attempting to be humorous."

"Jokes like that could hurt my trade," Bill grumbled. He scowled at the old crone contentedly sipping her glass of gin. "To be truthful she's a dreadful old cutthroat and I wouldn't have her inside my doors were it not for her connection with you, sir!"

"Blarney will get you nowhere!" the ancient Meg mocked him.

Bill remained scowling and turned to Jeremy. "Anything else, sir?"

"Not for the moment, Bill," Jeremy said suavely. "I have some things to discuss with these ladies. Perhaps you have business to attend to at the front of the house?"

The publican nodded his bald head and thumped back to the noisy bar section on his peg leg. This left the three of them alone in the dimly lighted back room. There was a silence between them for a little as they had their drinks.

Then Jeremy Quentain said, "As you can see, I have begun work on your case."

"Fortunately for me," she said.

"I came to the city tonight and stationed Meg, Alfie, and some of my other regulars about the house," he went on. "This pub is a sort of rendezvous for us when we're in this area. Bill is very tolerant about letting us use the place."

"He should be!" old Meg said with a twist of her sunken mouth. "Serving watered-down gin!"

Jeremy raised a hand to placate her. "I'm afraid that sort of talk can only cause us trouble, Meg. Whatever your thoughts, keep them to yourself!"

"Just as you say," Meg agreed reluctantly. "But when I buy for myself I look for an honest pub!"

Jeremy ignored this to give his attention to Adele again. "So you've finally come face to face with the Contessa?"

"Yes," she said.

"What do you think about her?" he wanted to know.

"She's beautiful, no arguing about that,"

Adele admitted. "But there is something very strange and sinister about her. And when she came out of her bedroom I think I saw something in there that confirms the whisperings about her."

"Oh?" Jeremy said, waiting to hear what this might be.

Adele hesitated. Then she said, "I'm almost certain I saw a coffin in the corner of her bedroom. It looked as if she might be using it to sleep in."

"Vampire style," Jeremy said with meaning.

"Yes," she agreed.

Old Meg spoke up. "There has to be something, sir. Nary a sign of her during the day. But come the dark and she's about."

"That fits the theory," Jeremy agreed. And he asked Adele, "What did she say to you about your brother?"

"She was very brazen," Adele told him worriedly. "She behaved as if she were sure she could keep her hold on him."

"Likely she can," the tall man said.

She gave him a frightened look. "What do you think she has done with him?"

"I don't know," he said. "But I do know he is somewhere in that house."

Adele shuddered. "I can't imagine where. Most of the house seems empty and deserted. They've just fixed up the apartment in which she holds forth."

"That suits their plan," Jeremy said. "Did you meet Carlos?"

"Yes. I thought at first he was merely a servant. But after a little I decided he had much more power than that."

"It seems likely. They say he was once the Contessa's lover; now he is in her employ."

"It's a bizarre place with frightening people," she said, her pretty face shadowed by the remembrance of it. "When Meg rescued me we were pursued by that awful Major and Carlos."

"They were bound to do that," Jeremy agreed. "And they won't be at all happy at having lost you. Without question they will try to make you their prisoner again. I can only hope that next time you won't be so co-operative."

Her cheeks burned with shame. "I deserve anything you say to me. I know it!"

"There is little use in my trying to help you unless you abide by my rules," the tall man warned her.

"You need not worry in future," she said.

"I hope I may have no reason," the tall man in the shabby outfit of Blind Paul said quietly. "In my opinion your brother is not going to return to you."

"Really?" she said, upset.

"I'm afraid the Contessa has him completely under her spell," Jeremy said. "My main object now will be to protect you and try to bring that wicked woman to some sort of justice."

"If you only can!" she said.

"I will try very hard," he assured her.

Bill came pounding in on his peg leg again and Jeremy had him go for another round of drinks for everyone. He told Adele, "A second sherry will do you no harm after your ordeal."

"As a matter of fact the one has made me feel a little better," she said.

Old Meg chuckled, the sunken eyes in the wrinkled face showing a merry gleam. "Gin is what you should cultivate, luv! It's a drink with real power, believe me!"

Jeremy said, "Gin is fine for you, Meg. You were raised on it. This young woman has been used to much weaker potions."

Meg smacked her sunken lips. "Gin is mother's milk to me!"

Jeremy turned to Adele again. "You probably find my being in disguise this way somewhat amusing."

"No," she protested. "I'm sure it is done for a good reason."

"Thank you for your confidence," he said.

"I try to hide my person when I'm engaged in these cases. If I became too well known a figure I would not be of much use as an investigator. So I occasionally adopt another role. Blind Paul is a useful one. No one pays too much attention to a blind man."

"I hadn't thought of that," she said. "But I suppose you are right. They aren't apt to worry about your spying on them."

"I've found that to be true," he said. "So Blind Paul serves me well. Now the next thing is to get you home safely. When Bill comes back with our drinks I'll have him go fetch you a cab."

And this was what he did. Within twenty minutes she was safely in a cab and back on the way to her home in the more fashionable part of London. She had left the ancient Meg and Jeremy in his tattered rags and black spectacles as Blind Paul behind in the rear of the Gull and Herring. She had no idea what they might have in mind for the rest of the night, but she now was aware of the scope of Jeremy Quentain's organization. It seemed he had half the underworld of London working with him.

Yet he felt dealing with the Contessa Maria Fillipio was not going to be all that easy. She shuddered as the cab rolled on over the cobblestoned streets, thinking that she might very well still be in that wretched, black room threatened by the rats. She had no idea what dreadful fate the Contessa had planned for her but she knew she had been fortunate to escape.

The cab delivered her safely to her door and when she entered old Marlow was there, looking weary, but still up waiting for her.

"I was sure you had fallen into misfortune," the old man said.

"I did have a brush with danger, but I managed to escape," she said. "Has my brother come home?"

"No sign of Mr. John," the old hunchback said. "I'd say he has left us for good this time."

"I hope not," she worried. "Surely he will come to his senses and realize that woman for the wicked creature she is."

Even as she said this and bade the old servant goodnight she knew it was unlikely her prediction would be correct. She went up to bed with a feeling of deep sadness. The only single thing which maintained her spirits was the knowledge that she had Jeremy Quentain on her side. As she lay waiting for sleep to come she thought about the handsome, melancholy man and his sad history.

Jeremy was surely one of the finest persons she had ever met, and he was also resourceful and determined. His battle with evil was an unending one according to legend. And since he had a suspicion that the Contessa was merely a puppet of the archcriminal, the Scorpion, it had whetted his interest in her case. It was a lucky day when she'd chosen at random the legal office of Oglethorpe and Huestiss and met Richard King, that pleasant young man who had taken her to Jeremy.

Now the face and figure of Richard King came vividly to mind. She had managed to become extremely fond of the young lawyer in the short time she'd known him. She felt he was a friend on whom she could depend. And he, in turn, appeared to have a genuine interest in her. She considered herself fortunate. But when she thought of him along with Jeremy Quentain, the young man faded somewhat. While she was grateful to Richard and fond of him, he was not the awe-inspiring figure Jeremy was.

She finally fell asleep thinking of these things. The night was uneventful. The following day was bright and much more pleasant. But as Johnny had still not returned she was overcome by gloom. And then around ten-thirty she received a message from the old lawyer who looked after their affairs in London. The old man urgently requested that she come to see him in his office at once. In his crabbed hand, he had written, "This matter has to do with your brother, John."

It was a summons she could not ignore. So she at once had Marlow call for the carriage while she went upstairs and found a bonnet and dress suitable for the visit to the lawyer's office. When she came down again and went out to get into the carriage she saw a fish peddler and heard him crying out that he had sole for sale, and she at once remembered that Jeremy had told her the man would be in her street to protect her.

Halting on the sidewalk she waited for the fish peddler with his barrow to come by. He was a thin youth with an upturned nose, freckled face, and a saucy smile. Seeing her he stopped and tipped his cap. "How about a nice sole, Miss? Very best sole!" He held one up.

"You are Alfie?" she asked.

"Right the first time, Miss," the youth said heartily.

She lowered her voice and said, "Let Mr. Quentain know that I have been called to my lawyer's. His name is Andrew Dodson and he has his office in Marboro Street."

"Right, Miss," the youthful fish peddler said. "A Dodson and a Marboro, a haddock and a bass! All the same to me, Miss! Shall I leave a sole at your door?"

"If you like," she said. "Ask for cook and say that I would like one baked and stuffed for dinner. And do see my message gets to Jeremy Quentain. It may have great importance."

Alfie winked at her. "One sole to cook! And a message to the mister! Depend on Alfie! I'll be around whenever you have need of me."

"Thank you," she said. And she left him to get into the carriage and begin the trip to the office of Lawyer Dodson.

She was greatly concerned about what the old lawyer might have to tell her. The message had said that it concerned Johnny, and that might mean anything. She felt somewhat better knowing that she had Jeremy Quentain on her side. The presence of the fish peddler on her street as Jeremy had promised made it clear he was doing all in his power to keep her safe.

Lawyer Dodson's office was in a street not far removed from the one where Richard King's office was located. The street had the same drab look as the other and boasted as many law offices. She had the carriage wait and went into the building where Andrew Dodson saw his clients. The office was a large one and his clerk was a stout, hearty young man.

He received her with a warm smile. "Ah, yes, Miss Foster. Mr. Dodson is expecting you. I'll take you directly in to him."

She followed the young man into the inner office where the overweight Andrew Dodson sat at his desk. He was a mammoth-sized man with a snowy head of hair and heavy black eyebrows. His face was like a moon with several chins. He rose to greet her with a deep sigh of effort and extended a pudgy hand.

"My dear Miss Foster," he wheezed. "So good of you to come so quickly."

She said, "I judged that the matter was urgent."

"And you were quite right," he said. "Do sit down!" He waved to a chair placed before his desk and she was quick to sit in it. He sank back into his own chair, which he overflowed, and leaned forward on his desk to study her worriedly.

Conscious of his troubled gaze, she said, "You suggested in the note this has something to do with my brother."

"Yes. I'm afraid so," the fat old man wheezed.

"Please let us get on with it, Mister Dodson," she pleaded with him.

The fat man's moon face took on a frown and his chins quivered. He told her, "I had a most unusual experience last night. I had retired to my bedchamber when my household was awakened by heavy poundings on the front door of my house."

"Really?"

"Yes," the old lawyer said. "And when I was called down to meet the intruder I found it to be your brother, John, and another party."

"Who was with him?" she asked.

The fat lawyer considered. "A middle-aged man whom I had never met before. Someone with a purplish complexion and sly look."

"That would be Major Merrithew."

"I believe your brother did call him Major," the fat man agreed with a nod of his white-haired head. The lively eyes under the heavy black brows fixed on her. "I had the two come into my study at home and I then enquired of your brother why he had come to my home rather than my office and why he was making the visit at a late hour in the night."

"What did he say?"

"He made no apology. Simply told me

that he wished to make a new will and have the Major witness it. I asked him about you and he said he had decided your share of the estate would look after you well enough. He had made up his mind to allot his half to a Contessa Maria Fillipio in the event of his sudden death."

Adele was not surprised by this news but it still was upsetting. She leaned back in her chair and asked him, "Did you not think this a strange business?"

"I did," Andrew Dodson said. "And I told your brother so. I advised him to give the matter further thought and come to my office later."

"And?"

"He wouldn't hear of it. He seemed in a strange, agitated mood, not at all like his usual self. He insisted that the will be drawn up then at his instruction. So I sat down with a pen and scratched off the words he dictated to me. Then he and this Major signed it."

She said, "So you have a signed and witnessed will giving my brother's inheritance to the Contessa Maria?"

"Yes."

Adele told him, "That evil woman has him in some sort of spell."

The fat man nodded. "I'm not at all surprised to hear that. John appeared different from the young man I had previously known. I could almost say that he seemed in a daze. His eyes were odd as if he were under the influence of some drug."

"He well might have been."

The fat man spread his hands in a gesture of resignation. "Yet I had no choice but to do his bidding. I have advised you at once as I'm sure you can reason with him. Wills can be set aside and new ones made. I suggest you talk earnestly with John and have him do this."

"He is not likely to. And I have a poor chance of seeing him and talking with him. He has left our house."

"Indeed?" Andrew Dodson showed concern.

"And I have no idea when he may come back. If ever."

"Most distressing!" the old lawyer sympathized. "Then one can only trust he will recover from this unfortunate infatuation and break with this Contessa on his own."

"I think there is only a small chance of that," she said.

The fat man frowned. "What can I do to help you, Miss Foster?"

"I doubt if there is anything beyond keeping me advised if my brother calls on you for services again."

"I shall surely do that."

Adele said, "I do have someone working in my behalf. Perhaps you may know him, a Jeremy Quentain."

The fat man's eyes widened. In a hushed tone he repeated the name, "Jeremy Quentain!"

"Then you do know him?"

Andrew Dodson looked troubled. "But, of course. He was once a fine trial lawyer. Perhaps the best in London. But lately he has given up his practice and taken to drugs and associating with figures in the underworld!"

She was startled by his words. "Surely you must be mistaken! I was told that he retired because of a personal tragedy. That his lovely young wife was murdered and he has made a vow to avenge her death."

The fat man looked impatient. "I believe his wife was struck down by thugs but I see no connection between that and what he has chosen to do with his life. I think the man a degenerate and I cannot advise that you have any association with him."

"You are serious?"

"Never more so," Andrew Dodson said. "Jeremy Quentain has made himself an outcast to his friends and his profession. Be wary of any offers of help from him."

"Thank you," she said quietly. But at the same time she took his words with a grain of salt. She knew that the conservative old lawyer would be bound to see Jeremy Quentain as a kind of outlaw. His comments in no way shook her faith.

"This is the year 1880, Miss Foster," the old lawyer said gravely. "London has grown into a large and wicked city. Not at all like it was in the days of my youth. Criminals lurk everywhere in the city streets now. You must beware of this evil. Constantly be on the alert."

"I will remember that," she told the old, fat man as she rose from her chair. "I will keep you no longer. Do get in touch with me if my brother contacts you again."

"At once, dear lady," Andrew Dodson said wheezily as he forced his huge bulk up once again. "Good day and good luck to you."

She thanked him and left the office. When she returned to her carriage she decided, since she was in the district, to stop by the office of Oglethorpe and Huestiss again and see young lawyer, Richard King. She was certain he would be interested in hearing this latest development concerning her brother. She told the driver where to take her and sat back on the carriage seat.

Now that John had legally willed his share of their estate to the Contessa it seemed likely things might develop quickly. The other two male victims of the Contessa had died soon after making bequests to her. There was no reason to expect that Johnny would not be treated in the same manner. Fear and sorrow fought for dominance within her as she worried about the fate of her beloved brother.

When she reached the office where she had first met Richard King the elderly clerk greeted her again. He went inside and when he came out Richard King was with him. The young lawyer came to her with a warm smile. "My dear Miss Foster," he said. "What a pleasant surprise!"

"I am not intruding on you at a busy time?" she worried.

"That is not important. I'm glad to see you," the pleasant young man enthused.

"I have come because I've just been to see my own lawyer, Andrew Dodson," she said. And then she went on to explain all that the fat man had told her, including his rather low opinion of Jeremy Quentain.

Richard King's young face showed grim amusement as he heard her comments. He said, "You may be sure that Andrew Dodson would not approve of Jeremy. None of the older men do. Not even my uncle. But I know Jeremy and I can promise you that you have made no mistake in allowing him to help you."

"That is how I feel," she agreed. "Last night I would have come to harm had he not been there to help me." And she briefly outlined her visit to the house of the Contessa.

"You were wrong to go there," Richard King told her.

"I know," she said. "It was foolish of me. I'll try to avoid making any other similar mistakes."

The young man eyed her worriedly. "I should hope so."

Before he could say anything more the door from the street opened and a remarkable-looking old man came shuffling in. He was on the stout side and well-dressed, though his gray frock coat and striped trousers had a look of not being pressed recently. His gray top hat was of the most expensive type and his cravat was gray with a fine diamond stickpin in it. But it was the face of the man that she found most striking: long, narrow, with a look of power. His lips were thick and his eyes were keen. And when he doffed his top hat his bald head arched high in a weird dome effect.

With an expression of pride on his young

face, Richard said, "May I introduce my uncle, Simon Oglethorpe? This is Miss Adele Foster whom I mentioned to you, Uncle."

Simon Oglethorpe bowed to her and in a rich, bass voice said, "You are the young American miss."

"Yes," she said. "Your nephew was kind enough to offer me help."

The old man with the slight stoop and high, domed bald head had a quizzical look on his narrow, stern face. "So he advised me. Though I question his judgement in sending you to Jeremy Quentain."

She said, "You are the second one to tell me that today. My family lawyer, Andrew Dodson, said somewhat the same thing."

Simon Oglethorpe nodded. "Andrew would be bound to share my dubious opinion of Jeremy Quentain's talents. I would think over Richard's advice, Miss Foster. You might be wise to avoid having contact with Jeremy Quentain at this sad date in his career. The man is an outcast."

"Thank you for your advice," she said.

The old lawyer eyed her bleakly and then turned to his nephew to tell him, "We have an acquittal in Higgins vs. The Crown. The jury gave their verdict only a half-hour ago."

"Congratulations, sir," Richard King said, seeming impressed.

His uncle shrugged. "I expected we'd win. I'll be in the office for a while now. I suggest you have your luncheon and take this young woman to the Strand. She looks as if a good meal would do her no harm. Young women are too thin today!" And he moved on to the door leading to the inner office and vanished.

Richard turned to her with an embarrassed smile, "Since my uncle has made the suggestion I cannot very well ignore it. Will you do me the honor of lunching with me again?"

She returned his smile. "I would enjoy it."

And so it was settled. And she was delighted to be in the company of the good-looking young lawyer once more. Richard King had come to mean a great deal to her in the short time she'd known him. It had seemed perfectly natural for her to visit him and give him the latest news about her problems.

They used her carriage to go to the Strand Restaurant. Then she dismissed the driver saying she would take a cab home. They were shown to a table in a remote corner of the fine restaurant where they could chat quietly.

Richard asked her, "How did you like my Uncle Simon?"

"He is an imposing figure," she said. "Rather odd, but he has a sense of strength and power about him."

"He is a fine lawyer," the young man said.

"I'm certain of it. Though I must say I can't agree with his opinion of Jeremy Quentain."

"Nor I," Richard said. "But I warned you before he arrived that he would think in the same fashion as Andrew Dodson. All the older men have the same opinion of Jeremy. And they are wrong."

"You seem certain of that."

"I am or I wouldn't have sent you to him," Richard told her.

They ordered, and the meal was excellent. When it was over they remained for a while at the table discussing her problem and also getting to know each other better. Richard invited her to attend a ball to be given by a legal colleague the following week, and she accepted.

She thoroughly enjoyed the luncheon. But when they rose to leave and she turned to walk out she saw the face of the man who had been seated at the table behind her. And she was shattered to find herself looking down into the bloated, purplish countenance of Major Merrithew. The Major returned her gaze with a sinister smile on his crafty face.

Chapter Six

Not until they had left the restaurant and were out on the busy sidewalk did she tell Richard about Major Merrithew. She quickly explained that he had been seated directly behind her and so must have heard everything they had discussed.

Richard King glanced back at the restaurant entrance with a troubled expression. "Should I go back inside and accuse the fellow of eavesdropping?" he worried.

"No," she said. "That would do no good. He'd only deny it and there's nothing we could prove. I just hope that we didn't say too much that he can use against us."

The young lawyer sighed. "Most of our conversation was personal."

"I'm glad of that," she said. "We had talked about my brother mostly at the office, that's on the credit side."

"I would try and forget all about it," the young man at her side advised.

She sighed. "Yes. I suppose I must. I

wonder if any of them will try to follow me home."

"We'll take care of that," Richard King said briskly. "I'll hail a cab and see you safely to your door."

"Oh, no, you mustn't! It will waste your time!" was her protest.

"I have time for this," Richard King insisted. "My uncle would be annoyed with me if I neglected you." And so despite her pleading he accompanied her home. He sat next to her in the cab with a worried expression on his pleasant young face. And as they arrived at their destination he took the opportunity of embracing her before he left the cab. They kissed in a most natural and friendly manner in parting.

She entered the old mansion with a warm feeling of happiness. At least out of this tragic business of Johnny there had emerged one good thing: her discovery of Richard King and the romance which was developing between them. She only wished that it was taking place under happier circumstances so she could more fully enjoy it. But even as things were, it was a pleasant development.

Marlow came to meet her and she could see the old hunchback was in no happier a mood than when she left. He informed her, "No sign of Mr. John, Miss."

"I don't expect we will hear from him for a while," she said.

"You think he's with that woman, Miss?" the old servant queried, the privilege of his years with the family allowing him to offer so personal a question.

"I'm afraid so," she said. "He visited Lawyer Dodson last night."

"Lawyer Dodson!" Marlow said in surprise.

She nodded and in a bitter voice said, "An urgent business of having his will changed. Of course he made a new will in favor of the Contessa."

"That is very serious, Miss," Marlow worried. "Your brother is behaving badly."

"He doesn't think so," she said. "We'll just have to wait and hope that he may come to his senses."

"Yes, Miss," the old hunchback said in an unhappy voice. "By the way, a lad came here selling fish. Said you had sent him. Cook bought a sole from him."

"I did send him," she agreed. "His name is Alfie. He may be around here regularly in the future."

"Just so long as you really did send him," Marlow said. "I told cook I would ask you."

After this exchange she went upstairs to

her room to rest for a little. As she changed into a robe for relaxing she was careful to keep the crucifix hung around her neck. She knew it would do little to protect her from the living evil but she was sure it would help her fight off any supernatural creatures which might threaten her.

She slept for a short while and her dreams were mostly of Jeremy Quentain and being rescued from evil forces by him. The quality of her nightmare was confused and the things which threatened her were not all that clear but always Jeremy was there to defend her. Her dream ended with a particularly vivid and frightening episode in which she came upon her brother sleeping on a sofa in a small, mean room. Then out of the shadows came a vampire Contessa to kneel in the shadowed area and place her mouth on John's throat.

The sight of the vampire draining her brother of his life's blood was so shocking that she screamed out. But neither John nor the Contessa seemed to see or hear her. It was as though she was watching the scene from another world. In a way she was. She came to in her own room aware that she'd been screaming in her sleep. Fortunately no one seemed to have heard her.

She rose and dressed. When she reached

the lower hallway a frowning Marlow was there to greet her. He said, "There's a person waiting in the sewing room, Miss. Said she had a message for you."

"Oh?" It was clearly apparent that Marlow didn't approve of the caller.

"Will you see her, Miss?" the hunchback queried her in a troubled tone.

"Is it an old woman who calls herself Meg?"

"Yes, Miss." The servant's tone was grim. "Scum of the streets if you ask me."

"It's all right, Marlow," she said. "I'll see her."

"I put her in the sewing room where there wasn't anything for her to steal," Marlow said. "You're sure you don't want me to call the police?"

"No, Marlow," she said. "These are upset times. Occasionally strange characters may come here asking for me. I want you to remember that most of them will be my friends. Treat them politely and let me know when they come."

The old hunchback looked shocked. "Yes, Miss, if that is what you wish."

"I'll go to the sewing room now," she said. "And will you be kind enough to bring in a tray with bottles of gin and sherry and glasses?"

"Gin and sherry?" His eyebrows raised.

She smiled, "It may sound an unlikely combination but I'm sure my visitor prefers gin while I enjoy sherry."

Having offered this explanation she left the flustered Marlow and went on down the hall to the sewing room. When she entered the room she saw old Meg standing there staring out the window with her back to her. It wasn't surprising that Marlow had doubts about the old woman, since she looked even more filthy and battered than on the previous night.

Adele said, "Hello, Meg. I didn't expect to see you so soon."

The old woman turned around quickly with an uneasy look on her wizened face. "Mister Jeremy sent me," she said.

"Did he?"

"Yes, Miss," the old woman said, clutching her ragged shawl to her bony shoulders and glancing around her nervously. "Is it safe to talk here, Miss?"

"It is."

Meg smacked her sunken lips and then said, "Mr. Jeremy says to tell you he knows about your brother having called on Lawyer Dodson last night."

She was amazed. "He does?"

"Yes, Miss," the old woman went on.

"He's going to try and get your brother out of that house tonight."

"How?" She was all interest.

The wizened face of old Meg showed a cautious look. "I can't tell you that, Miss. You'll have to wait to find out. But Mr. Jeremy has a plan. Not that he is sure that it will work."

"I see."

The ancient Meg pointed a thin forefinger at her and warned, "Most important, Mr. Jeremy says, is that you don't venture out of this house tonight."

"Very well, I won't," she promised.

"No matter what," the old woman said. "Not even if you get a message asking for you from your brother."

"I understand."

"Heed it," Meg said.

At that moment Marlow came in with the tray and bottles of gin and sherry, together with the needed glasses. He avoided looking at Meg as he set the tray down. This was fortunate as Meg was showing a wide smile of delight on her wizened face which would have shocked him further.

He gravely asked Adele, "Shall I serve, Miss?"

Adele did not wish to tax him further, so she said, "No. I will manage, thank you."

She waited until he had left the room and then she poured a full glass of gin for old Meg and passed it to her.

"Mother's milk!" Meg said happily. "You know my weakness!" And she downed a huge mouthful of the gin and her wizened face took on a happy glow.

Adele poured herself a small sherry to be hospitable. She sipped it and watched the old woman continuing to down the gin. She said, "Do you often deliver messages for Mr. Quentain?"

Meg wiped her lips with the back of her hand. "He trusts me more than the rest," she said.

"Does he have many other helpers?"

"He's got judys and lushingtons and didikis working for him along with a lot of others," the old woman said knowingly.

Adele stared at her in blank astonishment. "I don't think I understand you. What are judys?"

"Pretty girls, streetwalkers," Meg said with disgust. "I was never one of them. I had a good husband, I did. Taught me a bit about pickin' pockets, that man did. Cut off in his prime by pneumonia but I never have forgotten all that he taught me."

"You're still a pickpocket?"

Meg finished her gin. "When I'm not employed by Mr. Quentain. He has me fair tied up a lot of the time."

"What are lushingtons and didikis whom you mentioned?"

"Drunks and gypsies," the old woman said patronizingly. "You don't know much, do you?"

"Not about such things," she admitted.

Meg thrust her empty glass at her. "Another one for the road, luv."

She took the glass and asked, "Aren't you afraid of getting drunk and having something happen to you?"

The wizened old Meg laughed loudly. "Me, drunk? You're not about to see that happen, my girl. Not when what runs in my veins is half blood and half gin. My mother suckled me on the Embankment with a bottle to her lips. Natural to me, gin is!"

Adele poured a somewhat smaller second helping and gave it to the crone. Meg blinked at it with mild disappointment but she downed the burning, colorless liquor without a word.

Adele said, "When will I see Jeremy Quentain again?"

Meg shrugged. "I can't tell you that. Best I be on my way. I have important tasks ahead for the night."

Adele thanked her and saw her to the

door. The old woman went hurrying off down the street with an agility rare in one of her age. Adele thought the gin might have something to do with it. Again she was startled by the way Jeremy Quentain had of finding things out. And she prayed that he might somehow get to her brother and free him from the evil Contessa.

That evening was a long, grim one for Adele. After dinner she read for a while. Then she went up to bed early but she was not able to sleep. She kept thinking about Johnny and the danger he was in. And the more she considered it all the more she felt he was not liable to escape the clutches of the Contessa and her crowd alive. He was all too probably slated to be their third victim. And who would be next? Perhaps she might be the next object of their attack. It was a terrifying business, even with Richard and Jeremy to aid her, and she wished it was at an end.

Finally she sank into an uneasy sleep — and awoke with a start!

The room was in darkness and she knew that it was about the middle of the night though she had no actual idea of what the hour might be. She was awake and filled with fear! Fear for which she could give no reason! She raised herself on an elbow and peered at the shadows of the room for a sign of movement.

There was none. And yet she had this feeling that she was not alone. That there was a threatening presence somewhere in that room with her. Her heart was beating rapidly and she was covered with a cold, clammy sweat. She was about to reach out and try to light the candle on her bedside table when she heard a rustling from the far corner of the room.

This froze her with terror. Her eyes widened and she renewed her study of the shadows. And then gradually she saw a form take shape. Someone was standing there in the darkness. The figure moved and started coming slowly towards her. She began to sob with fright; her teeth were chattering and she clutched at the bedcovering with frozen hands.

The figure came nearer. And to her utter surprise she saw that it was her brother, Johnny!

"Johnny!" she called out in relief. "You've come back!"

He did not reply but merely stared down at her with a tragic look on his face. He seemed unable to speak. But he came a little closer to her with each passing second.

Her relief began to dissolve into new fears

as she saw his weird eyes, his set, sad expression, and noted his mad, stony silence.

She cried, "Johnny! Why don't you speak to me?"

His response to this was to look even more sad and open his mouth without uttering a word. Then her eyes fixed on his lips which seemed abnormally thick and on his teeth which were a menacing white, and a new kind of terror shot through her.

"My God!" she screamed and she groped for the crucifix which she had left on the bedside table.

At the same time he was bending down over her so that she could smell his fetid breath. She twisted in bed to escape those threatening teeth, certain that given the chance he would sink them in her throat. He now uttered a snarling sound and reached for her. But she had found the crucifix and with a quick movement she brought it up directly before him.

The reaction on his part was immediate. His good-looking face took on an unholy expression of fear. He reached up to his throat with his hands and made a choking noise, as if unseen fingers were clutching at him and shutting off his breath. Then he stumbled backward into the shadows and was lost to her.

Even as he vanished she knew that she had wanted to talk to him. Terrified as she'd been, she had hoped to quiet him with the crucifix and then try to reason with him. But he had gone as quickly as he'd appeared. She sat up in bed with the crucifix still held before her as protection. The room was silent again as if no one had ever been there.

But she knew Johnny had been there. She hurriedly draped the crucifix around her throat and then groped for matches and the candle. When she had the candle lit she got up from her bed and put on a robe and slippers. With the candle in her hand she set out to find her brother.

She had no doubt that he'd been hypnotized in some way by the Contessa. But in spite of her fear of him she had hoped to try and reason with him. Now she moved quickly out of the dark room and along the corridor to her brother's bedroom, the small flame from the candle she carried supplying the only glow of light in the eerie blackness of the old house.

She reached her brother's door and saw that it was partly ajar. Her hopes were aroused that he might still be there, she pushed open the door and called out, "Johnny!"

There was no reply, just a mocking silence

from the dark bedroom. She took a further step in and called out again, "Johnny, please answer me if you're there! I want to talk with you!"

But only silence came from the shadows. She stood there not knowing what to do. Then she went rigid as she heard a footstep behind her. She stood there not daring to turn around.

"Miss Adele," a worried voice said. And she knew it was that of Marlow.

She turned to see the old hunchback in dark robe and white nightcap. He was also carrying a lighted candle and he asked her, "What are you doing up at this hour, Miss?"

A concerned look on her pretty face, she told him, "My brother came into my room a few minutes ago."

His eyes widened. "Mr. Johnny?"

"Yes. He must be here somewhere."

"You're certain, Miss?"

"I tell you I saw him," she said impatiently. "I thought he might have come in here."

The old man went the rounds of the room, then he told her, "No one here, Miss."

"We'll search the rest of the house. He must be somewhere around," she insisted.

The old servant was gazing at her

strangely as he asked, "Are you sure that you didn't dream your brother was here, Miss?"

"No," she said sharply. "Keep up the search for him."

The search went on. She and Marlow covered every corner of the house without discovering a sign of her brother. There was not even any evidence that he had entered the house. Both the front and rear doors remained locked and latched. She could see that Marlow felt it had been a nightmare on her part and she was dreadfully embarrassed. But in the end she had no choice but to admit defeat and give up.

In a dull voice, she said, "We may as well go back to our beds, Marlow."

"As you say, Miss," the old man sighed.

"I did see my brother but he must have left before we began our search."

"Yes, Miss," the old man said.

She knew that out of consideration for her he wasn't asking the awkward questions about the locked doors and why nothing had been disturbed. She went to her bedroom feeling shamed and worried. And for the balance of the night she left the candle burning in its holder and kept the crucifix around her neck.

In the morning she awoke with a bad headache and a feeling of gloom. She saw that during the night fog had crept over the city. Outside the thick gray mist obscured a view of anything more than a few feet distant. The mood of the morning matched her own. She washed and dressed for breakfast and then went downstairs.

She'd barely finished her breakfast when she heard someone at the front door. Marlow answered the door and then came for her. The old hunchback looked shaken as he said, "Someone at the door. I think you had better come, Miss."

She followed him out to the entrance hall thinking that it might be one of Jeremy Quentain's ragged underworld messengers waiting to see her, but feeling uneasily that it must be something more than that. Something to do with her brother. The memory of last night was still vivid.

When she reached the open door she had difficulty hiding her shock. Standing there patiently were a man in a shabby blue suit and top hat and a policeman in official uniform. The man in the blue suit was on the elderly side and had a large gray mustache. He doffed his hat and bowed to her respectfully.

"Miss Adele Foster?" he asked in a rather hoarse voice.

"Yes," she said timorously, conscious that the policeman was watching them both.

"I have come here on a rather sad errand," the man with the mustache said. "You must prepare yourself for a shock, Miss."

"What is it?" she asked in a taut voice.

"Your brother, Miss," he said.

"Yes?"

He sighed and shuffled his feet a little. "No easy way to put it, Miss. Your brother is dead."

She gripped the door handle and tried to brace herself against fainting. "No!" she protested.

"I'm afraid so, Miss. We found one Mr. John Foster, lately of New York City, American citizen, in the bed of a cheap lodging house in the East End this morning."

"You can't have! He was here last night!" she protested weakly.

The man with the mustache looked grave. "We have all his papers, Miss. They were still on him. There's little chance of our having made a mistake."

She shook her head. "Not John!"

"I'm sorry, Miss," the man said. "The proprietor of the place claims your brother came in late last night and seemed to have been drinking a lot. He paid for his bed and that was the last time anyone seems to have seen him alive. He died in his sleep as you might say. No suffering at all, is my guess. That is something to be thankful for, Miss."

His voice came to her like a kind of weird echo as she asked him, "What do you want of me?"

"Matter of final identification," the mustached one said awkwardly. "If you will come with this officer and myself to make sure he is your brother we'll then be able to turn the body over to you for burial."

Her eyes were blurred with tears. "You want me to come with you now?"

"If you will, Miss," the man said. "Better to get it done and over with I'd say."

Marlow had come out to stand by her and said, "If you wish I'll accompany you and the officer, Miss."

She gave the old hunchback a grateful look. "If you would, Marlow. I'm not sure I can stand the ordeal alone."

And she was quite right. It was an ordeal. She and the old servant went with the two from the police department in the plain carriage which had been provided. In a room given over to the dead the mustached man pulled back a sheet from over a body resting on a slab and she saw Johnny's placid white face. His eyes were staring and there could be no question he was dead. She turned away with a sob.

The mustached man followed her, "Now about the funeral arrangements, Miss. Whom do you wish to take the body?"

"Let me think," she said, tears brimming over her eyes.

"Yes, Miss," the man in blue said, escorting her back to the main room of the district police station.

She no sooner was in this room with the mortuary door closed behind her than she saw a familiar figure waiting for her. It was Jeremy Quentain who stood there in his dark suit, with a cloak draped around his shoulders and wearing his deerstalker hat. The tall, thin man came across to her and placed a comforting arm around her.

"You mustn't give way to grief," he said. "Not at this moment. We have too much to do."

She raised her tear-filled eyes to give him a questioning look. "How did you find out?"

Jeremy's handsome face looked more melancholy than usual. Quietly, he said, "I was told."

"What am I to do?" she asked.

"I will take you home," Jeremy said. "One of my men will be here in a few minutes to look after the funeral arrangements. When the body is ready he will bring it to your house to remain there until the funeral."

"You are looking after everything, then?" she asked.

"Everything," he said. And he told Marlow, "I have a cab waiting for us outside. We will all ride back together."

So it was Jeremy who came to her aid at the worst moment of crisis and saw her safely home. Never had she been more grateful for the tall, handsome man's aid. Little was said in the carriage between them. But little needed to be said. She had complete faith in the melancholy Jeremy and knew she could trust him completely.

In the living room she sat with bowed head on a divan while Jeremy paced back and forth before her. Now that she was home she attempted to cope with the reality of John's death. There was no use trying to run from it. Nothing would change.

She said, "I find it hard to believe. I saw him here in my room last night."

Jeremy stopped pacing and stared at her with a questioning look on his lean, handsome face. "Tell me all about it."

She did ending with, "When we tried to find him he had gone."

Jeremy gave her a meaningful look. "If he were ever truly here?"

Adele hesitated. "You're not trying to say

it was some kind of nightmare? It was too real!"

"I didn't mention a nightmare."

"What then?"

He sighed. "Everything you say suggests that your brother was not by any means his normal self. I suggest you must have felt this or you would not have reached out for the crucifix."

"True," she admitted. "But I put that down to the evil that woman had instilled in him. I'm certain I could have reasoned with him."

"I wonder," Jeremy said.

"What do you mean?"

"According to the police your brother checked into that cheap lodging house in some kind of strange state. Later he died. I'd be willing to bet when the body is brought here you will see two tiny scars on his neck. The same sort of scars found on the throats of those other two men who gave their fortunes to Contessa Maria in their wills."

With a look of horror on her lovely face she rose quickly. She exclaimed, "You're saying my brother did not die a natural death!"

"I'm afraid we must consider that."

"The police seem satisfied that he died of

heart failure or some such natural cause," she pointed out.

Jeremy said, "No doubt his heart did fail him. But I would like to know the cause of its failure. I think it came from evil forces outside him."

Her eyes met his piercing ones. "I fully agree," she said. "I have to believe that the Contessa was the one who brought about his death. Either she or her agents!"

"Quite likely."

"So John became the third victim of her greed! She must not benefit from that will they tricked him into making!"

Jeremy said, "His death did come conveniently soon after it."

"How can we fight them?"

He said, "It is bound to be difficult."

She gave him a pleading look. "You can win them over, Jeremy. I can't do anything alone. But with your aid I know it will be all right. I trust you, Jeremy! I believe in you!"

The tall man's handsome face took on a new glow at her words. He said, "I have already pledged myself to help you. Thus far I feel I have failed. I should have saved your brother's life. Too late for that now. But I swear that I will protect you. Perhaps you have guessed, I have a deep affection for you, Adele!" And he drew her to him slowly and gently touched his lips to hers.

It was a brief kiss filled with meaning. She had always had faith in him but never more so than at this moment. And she knew her reverence for him was akin to love.

He released her with a shadow of regret on his handsome face and said, "I should not have done that."

"You have heard no complaint from me," Adele told him.

"I know," he said. "But it was not fair of me at this time. You are still in a state of shock. Your brother's death has naturally upset you."

She gave a deep sigh. "Perhaps not as much as I expected. In a way I knew it was going to happen. I could see it was what he was heading for and yet I didn't know how to help him."

"You tried."

"I did my best," she said, with a tragic shrug. "It wasn't enough."

"Apparently," Jeremy said, looking thoughtful. "Now we must try to save *you* from those people."

She stared up at him. "You think they will not be satisfied? That they will continue to bother me?"

"Yes. Especially if you try to stand between them and the fortune your brother left them."

"I intend to!" she said. "If there is any means of keeping them from that money I must use it."

"You can appeal. Contest the will. A good lawyer can help you fight them."

"Richard King," she suggested.

"He can do it," Jeremy agreed. "But there is another area in which it will be more difficult to protect you. We know the Contessa has the reputation of being involved in black magic. If she should also be a vampire as we suspect, you may be open to attack by the supernatural."

"You think my brother's death may have been brought on by his being a victim of a vampire?"

"I do," Jeremy replied. "And unless you had an extremely vivid nightmare last night, the figure of your brother, which you insist entered your room, had to be a ghost or a vampire."

Fear shadowed her lovely face. "I did see him clearly and I thought he was very different! Strange! Almost menacing!"

"That fits," Jeremy said quietly, "since it is my fear that the vampire curse has been passed on to your brother and he was sent here to attack you last night."

Chapter Seven

Horror surged through Adele as she listened to the solemn words of Jeremy Quentain. It had never occurred to her that the Contessa might select John as her evil messenger. But as she recalled the peculiar look of her brother the night before she could understand that the possibility of his being a vampire intent on her murder might not be so improbable.

She said, "I can't believe that John would ever harm me. Not even under that woman's spell."

Jeremy sighed. "I hope you are right, but I could not ignore the possibility."

"John is dead," she said. "Let us pray they can do no more to him."

"I agree that making him a slave beyond the grave would be the most dreadful thing of all."

She gave him an anxious look. "You say that the undertaker who will prepare his body and bring it here to rest until the funeral is a friend of yours."

"Yes, he is a man I can trust. His name is Henry Dover, in case he should arrive with the body when I'm not here."

She gave a tiny shudder. "Do you think the body will be safe?"

"I have thought about that," Jeremy said. "And I've also worried over your safety with the presence of a possible vampire here in the house, for we cannot rule that out."

"I'll be all right," she said.

"Don't be too sure," he warned her. "Best that we have a person on guard by the coffin all the time. I shall call at Henry Dover's undertaking establishment and discuss this with him. I'll suggest that he and his helper take turns in doing guard duty."

Jeremy left soon after this discussion and she at once felt more bleak and deserted. The handsome man had a way of bolstering her courage. She decided that she should let Richard King know about her brother's death and so she wrote him a brief note and gave it to Marlow to deliver to him.

The day seemed endless. There was no respite from the fog and cold. She was standing alone in the drawing room shivering when Marlow returned and at once started a fire in the great marble fireplace.

She asked him, "Did you reach Mr. King?"

The old hunchback paused before her respectfully. "No, Miss. He was out of the office when I called there. I understood from his clerk that he had gone to lunch. I left the note with the clerk."

"That was the wise thing," she agreed.

Marlow's wizened face was sad. "To think that Mr. John is dead. After you fought so hard to save him."

"I'm afraid it was an unequal battle, Marlow," she said.

"Evil people! They can be the ruin of anyone, Miss," Marlow said unhappily. "The rest of the household wish me to express their deep sympathy for you."

"Thank you," she said. "Tell them I am most grateful."

The old man hesitated and then asked, "Will you be bringing the body of Mr. John here?"

"Yes," she said. "The undertaker has taken his body from the police station and is preparing it in a proper casket now. It should soon arrive."

At that moment there was a knocking at the front door and Marlow left her to answer it. She stood waiting tensely thinking it might be the body arriving. Marlow returned a moment later with a troubled look.

"There is a man here to see you, Miss," he

said in his quavering voice. "A man I have not seen before."

She frowned. "Didn't he give his name?"

"No."

"Can it be the undertaker? Is there a hearse outside?"

"No, Miss. And I do not think this man is the undertaker. He is a rather arrogant sort of person."

"I'd better see him," she worried, thinking it might be someone Jeremy had sent.

Marlow said, "Then I shall show him in?"

"Yes, please," she said, still wondering who it might be.

A moment later a man in a black cape entered the drawing room and came slowly to stand in front of her. It was Carlos, as erect in bearing and as arrogant as on that other occasion when she had met him at the Contessa's house.

His pale, distinguished face had a somber look as he said, "I have come to express our sympathy in the death of your brother. Contessa Fillipio asked that you be told she shares your sorrow."

"Indeed," Adele said quietly. The appearance of the man had made her fear she might faint.

"Your brother's sudden death must have been a shock," Carlos said.

She stared at him. "How could you know he is dead unless you had something to do with it?"

The dignified, white-haired man drew himself up in shocked amazement. "The fact of his death is generally known in the city."

"That is not true," she said sharply. "Who exactly told you?"

Carlos looked uneasy. "I cannot truly remember. It was such shattering news."

Adele's angry grief could not be contained. "She had him killed and then sent you here to see my sorrow!"

"That is an unjust accusation," Carlos sputtered. "The Contessa is a great lady. Her love for your brother was widely heralded."

"She was in love with his estate," Adele snapped back. "I know about the will!"

"Indeed?" Carlos said with an unpleasant smile. "That will make things less complicated."

"Don't think that!"

"Your brother informed me he had left the Contessa all his estate," Carlos told her. "And that will surely mean half this fine house. May I say the Contessa is seeking a more suitable residence and it is possible she may be interested in this place!"

"How dare you!" she cried. "My brother hardly dead and you come with this talk!"

"Please!" He raised a restraining hand. "I'm merely telling you that the Contessa would be quite willing to buy the other half of this house from you. Naturally you'll be going back to America. I think it could be an excellent solution for you."

"That is kind of you!" she said bitterly. "Especially under the circumstances!"

"The Contessa's intentions are most generous," Carlos said with a cold smile.

"Let me warn you I intend to contest the will!" she cried. "I will fight it to the highest court before I see you get a sovereign of my brother's money!"

Carlos shrugged under his black cape. "That would be most unwise."

"Unwise or not, that is my intention," she stormed.

Carlos eyed her with disdain. He said, "Please remember this, nothing you can do will change things. Better to accept what has happened and avoid any danger to yourself."

"Is that a threat?"

He shrugged again. "Make of it what you will."

"I'm not alone," she told him. "I have a friend who will help me deal with you."

"I trust your friend is a man of some power."

"I'm sure you've heard of him. His name is Jeremy Quentain!"

"Quentain!" Carlos said, and for a brief moment he showed uneasiness. Then he quickly covered this with another of his cold smiles as he asked, "Do you mean the lawyer who was disbarred?"

"I know nothing about that," she said. "But I do know the man and I think he is a match for you!"

"Interesting," Carlos said with all his poise returned. "I think your Jeremy Quentain is known mostly for his opium addiction and the madness it has brought on. Do not count on him!"

"Please leave this house," she commanded the white-haired Carlos.

He bowed. "If that is your wish. Again the Contessa shares your grief. And you will be hearing from her lawyers very shortly. Good day, Miss Foster!" With that he turned and stalked out.

She stood staring after him, livid with anger. Then when she heard the door close after him all her pent-up emotion burst forth and she began to sob violently. She sought an easy chair and buried her face in her handkerchief. The exchange had been a humiliating and frustrating experience and had left her emotionally shattered. It had been almost as if the Contessa had come to triumph over her.

She was still huddled in her chair when Marlow came into the room. He placed the silver tea tray on a table near her and stood waiting in sympathetic silence. Adele hastily dabbed at her eyes and sat up straight.

"I've been indulging my grief, Marlow," she told the hunchback.

The old servant said, "You are entitled to your grief. It is nature's means of allowing us to endure tragedy."

"Thank you, Marlow," she said. "That man who was here just now is evil. His name is Carlos and he is in the employ of the Contessa. If he calls again do not let him in."

"Very well, Miss," the old man said. "I brought you some tea."

"That is very good of you," she told him. And she poured herself a strong cup of the steaming liquid. Somehow sipping it made her feel better.

And it was then that Richard King arrived. The young man was shown in by a pleased Marlow and came to her hurriedly. He took her in his arms as she rose from her chair and gazed at her with deep sympathy.

"My poor Adele! I received your note when I came back to the office. How dreadful for you!"

"I wanted you to know," she said.

"Of course," Richard said. "Now tell me what happened and when."

They sat down and she told him all that she knew. Then they discussed this over tea. Richard King said, "By the way, my Uncle Simon was upset by your news. He sent his deepest condolences to you."

"Dear Mr. Oglethorpe!" she said.

"He is a kindly man by nature," Richard agreed. "Now that he is getting older he is less thoughtful than he used to be. But he has a great deal on his mind. One important case after another."

"I understand," she said.

Richard said, "Now you are alone. We must all try to take care of you."

"John was not all that much comfort," she said. "Especially not lately. Not since the Contessa came into his life."

"And seemingly brought about his death," Richard said grimly.

"I'm sure they deliberately killed him."

"But in some manner so that it seemed a natural death," he said.

"The police were completely taken in," she admitted worriedly. "I don't suppose they'd listen to any charges against the Contessa."

"Not unless you had some solid proof."

"And I haven't."

"So?"

She gave Richard a knowing glance. "It will all have to depend on Jeremy Quentain. He is the only one who can make them pay for what they've done."

Richard looked sober. "I hope he may be able to do that. I was the one who suggested him to you."

"For which I will be forever grateful."

"Do you two get along well?"

"Yes," she said. "I'm extremely fond of him."

"Fond?" Richard showed surprise.

"I mean I admire him greatly and I have every confidence in him," she hastened to say.

Richard seemed to agree with this. He said, "I would expect that." He took his watch from his vest pocket and consulted it. "I must return to my office. I have a client coming to visit me. You say that the undertaker is bringing your brother's body here?"

"Yes," she said. "It was good of you to come. Do hurry along. I don't want to keep you late." She got to her feet to see him to the door.

As they walked to the door, he had his arm linked in hers and held her hand. He said, "I don't want you to think that Jeremy Quentain is your only friend."

Gazing up at the young lawyer, she said, "You know that I don't!"

Richard smiled. "From the moment of our first meeting I have always felt that we were meant for each other."

"I believe my going to your office was the most important decision I made in my life," she said.

He halted by the door. "This is not a time to discuss such things. But let me say, I don't want to lose you to Jeremy. He has a great deal of charm but I doubt that he would ever be happy in a second marriage and I would not want your life spoiled for you."

She blushed at his words. "Whoever thought of such a thing? I regard Jeremy as my friend. I have never considered him in a romantic way. Just now I need him so because of poor John."

"I understand," Richard said. "And it was I who brought you two together. I felt I should speak frankly because you and Jeremy will be seeing a great deal of each other. You will come to depend on him. But you mustn't lose your heart to him. I do not think I could bear that."

"Richard!" she said softly.

The young lawyer kissed her on the forehead. Then he said, "I will return this evening when your brother's body is here. I hope Jeremy is taking precautions for your safety?"

"He is," she assured him, and sent him on his way.

Now the day was coming to a close. A day of tragedy which she would never forget. The mortuary at the police station was an aspect of London which she had never encountered before and which she would have been satisfied not to have encountered at all. She thought she would never be able to forget that ugly moment when the attendant had thrown back the sheet and allowed her to see John's pale, fixed countenance.

Her brother had drifted away from her in London. His drinking had tended to cause this schism between them even before they left New York. But with London and the Contessa he became almost like a stranger with her. While she mourned him her mourning was tempered by this knowledge. She feared that had he been allowed to live he might have sunk to the limits of degradation.

But that did not make his murder acceptable to her. For murder she believed it to be. And the visit of Carlos had proven that the Contessa knew all about it and was greedily waiting to collect her share of the estate. She even had her eye on this house in which Adele was living. It was too much!

Then there was this other business! The question of whether the Contessa and her henchmen had gone beyond the limits of black magic and were in the area of the supernatural. Was the Contessa a vampire? And had John been struck down by an attack on the part of this creature? If so, would he be forever tainted with the vampire curse? Wasn't there some way to break it? She touched the crucifix she was wearing with nervous fingers and tried to remember what she'd read somewhere.

A stake through the heart! She was sure that somewhere she had read of this as the sure way to destroy a vampire. Could she summon the resolution to have someone drive a stake through her brother's heart as he lay in his coffin? It would be the one sure way to save him from carrying out the Contessa's bidding if he'd been tainted by the vampire curse!

But what a cruel and pointless thing to do if he had not been turned into a vampire. Dare she allow him to be buried in an ordinary way? She knew that vampires were supposed to be able to escape from the grave. And again she recalled his macabre appearance when he'd emerged from the shadows of her room the other night. She had the sickly fear that if she'd not produced the crucifix he would have made straight for her throat in a vampire attack.

It presented her with an eerie problem. She could only hope that Jeremy Quentain would help her face this gruesome situation. And this made her wonder why she had not heard from the tall, dark man or the undertaker who he'd promised would shortly arrive with John's body. It was getting dark and so far there had been no word from Jeremy or the undertaker.

Marlow came into the drawing room with two lighted lamps and set them out. "What do you wish for dinner, Miss?"

"I'm not hungry, Marlow," she said. "Perhaps a cup of consommé and some crackers."

"Nothing else?"

"No," she said. "Bring it here on a tray. I'm expecting the undertaker soon. He should have been here by now."

"It is getting late, Miss," Marlow agreed and went out to get her the light food she'd ordered.

But before Marlow could return with her food there was an unexpected interruption. It began with a loud knocking on the front door and because she was close by it, Adele answered it herself. When she opened the door she saw standing there, wreathed in thick mist, one of the oddest-looking men she had ever seen.

In a faint voice, she said, "Yes?"

"I'm the undertaker, Miss," the macabre figure on the doorstep said, doffing a battered black top hat to reveal a bald head with some dark strings of hair matted across it. The man was weirdly thin with deep hollows in his cheeks and sunken eyes with a weird gleam in them.

She said, "Did Mr. Quentain send you?"

"Yes, Miss," the scarecrow figure in black said.

She glanced out into the street and saw only a carriage. She then asked him, "Where is the hearse with my brother's body?"

The undertaker said, "That is my message, Miss. Mr. Quentain decided it would be best not to bring the deceased here."

"Oh?"

"Yes, Miss," the undertaker went on. "So on Mr. Quentain's orders I took the body directly to St. Dunstan's Cemetery, which is not too far from here; they have a vault there to keep the body until you select a lot for burial."

She was baffled by it all. "You took my brother directly to the cemetery?"

The undertaker tapped the side of his nose with a wise look on his emaciated face. "Precaution, Miss. Mr. Quentain didn't want to risk the body being interfered with, if you know what I mean?"

"I think I do," she said. "Of course this changes everything."

"It does, Miss. And may I say your brother looks very natural. I worked on him myself. You'll be pleased."

"I'm glad to hear it," she said faintly. She had just become aware of the heavy smell of whiskey on the undertaker's breath. She was not all that surprised as she'd been told it was a weakness of the profession. Undertakers, because of their dismal work, were prone to drink heavily.

He said, "Mr. Quentain would like you to join him at St. Dunstan's."

"The cemetery?"

"Yes, Miss. He felt you would like to see the body and the casket and all."

"I would," she agreed. "I expected you'd be here with the body at any moment."

"The change in plans caused the delay,"

the undertaker said. "But I think it is for the best."

"If Mr. Quentain thinks so."

"He does, Miss," the undertaker said. "He would have come for you himself but he said he wanted to stay by the body. He seems afraid that someone will wish to do it harm."

"I understand that," she said. "And you say he is at St. Dunstan's now, waiting for me?"

"That he is, Miss," the undertaker said. "I have a carriage to take you there. It won't be too long a journey."

"Very well," she said. "It's still cold and foggy so I'll get my cloak."

"You'll need it, Miss. I found it fair raw in the cemetery," the undertaker said.

She hurried and got her cloak and was on her way out just as Marlow returned with the tray. She said, "I can't wait for that now. I have to meet Mr. Quentain at St. Dunstan's cemetery. They've taken my brother there."

"But why?" the old man asked in surprise, the tray in his hands.

"It would take too long to explain," she said. "But it is Mr. Quentain's idea. I'm sure it is all right."

"Very well, Miss," Marlow said with a hint of distress in his tone.

She went outside and joined the under-taker. She asked him, "Will Mr. Quentain be waiting at the vault?"

"When I left him he was inside it, Miss. Standing by your brother's casket, he was. He's a fine man, Miss."

"I couldn't agree more," she said.

The scarecrow figure of the undertaker hurriedly helped her into the cab and then got up front to take the reins. In a moment they were on their way.

The cab reeked of stale cigar smoke and cheap scent. Adele decided the mourners who had last used it must have been of the sporting class. She realized that it took all kinds of people to make the world and the undertaker had to cater to a wide mixture of them.

Settling back against the horsehair seat she tried to relax. But she was in much too upset a state. She wondered why Jeremy had decided to make a change in the fu-neral arrangements and felt sure it had something to do with the Contessa and her evil group.

The cab rattled through the streets and she had fleeting glimpses of shops with their lights only a yellow blur through the fog. The gray mist had become so thick you could only see a few feet in any direction clearly. Because the interior of the cab was damp and cold she shivered.

The cab rolled on and left the streets with lights behind. Adele had no idea where they were or even where St. Dunstan's Cemetery was located. She suspected it would be served by a church of the same name. And she wondered whether it might be possible to hold a funeral service for her brother in the nearby church. The idea appealed to her.

Suddenly the cab came to a halt and after a moment the thin undertaker opened the cab door and helped her out. "Trust the drive wasn't too hard on you, Miss?" he enquired.

Clinging to the side of the cab she reached out for the hand of the undertaker and he helped her down onto a pathway. The fog was so dense she could see nothing but the billowing clouds of it around them.

She asked him, "Where do we go now?"

"It's not far from here," the undertaker assured her as he led the way on his spindly legs.

She asked him, "Are you Mr. Dover?"

He said, "No. Mr. Dover was engaged so Mr. Quentain had me do the job. I've worked for Mr. Quentain before. He's a generous man."

"I agree," she said. As they walked along

the path in the fog she realized how isolated she was. She also saw how completely she had placed herself in the care of the undertaker. But he was sure to be trustworthy since Jeremy had picked him.

"This is a quiet cemetery," she said, as she brushed by a wet border of shrubs.

"Just a moment now," the undertaker puffed, seeming weary from his walking.

And she saw that they were in a cemetery area. To the left and ahead of her the gravestones rose up like bleak sentinels. She felt a growing fear well up in her and wished that they would get to their destination. She needed the presence of Jeremy and his reassurance to give her confidence.

"Where is the vault?" she asked her strange guide.

The scarecrow undertaker halted and turned to her. "It is just over there," he told her. "We can pick our way through the gravestones."

They walked across the rows of graves and finally reached a square marble structure with heavy iron doors. The doors showed signs of rust and were closed against the foggy night.

Surprised, she asked her guide, "Is Jeremy Quentain in there?"

"With your brother's body," the undertaker said. He drew back one of the iron doors. It opened with a weird scraping noise to reveal a dark, dungeonlike area inside. "In there," he told her.

"Are you coming with me?"

"No. I'll wait out here," he said.

She glanced in at the dark dungeon again and took a deep breath. She hated going into the black, eerie place but she knew she had a duty towards her brother and she desperately wanted to speak with Jeremy. So she slowly stepped inside the vault and peered into the shadows.

There were coffins stacked on shelves on either side of the vault and a distance ahead she saw a dark-garbed figure which she took to be Jeremy.

"Jeremy!" she called out his name and took several hurried steps towards the man with his back to her.

As she came up to him he slowly turned and she saw revealed the bloated, evil face of Major Merrithew. In his suave voice, he said, "Good evening, Miss Foster!"

"You!"

"You are surprised to see me here?" he asked.

"I came to meet Mr. Quentain and see my brother's body," she said. "What are you doing here?"

Major Merrithew's smile was mocking. "Surely you don't question my right to be here?"

"Where is Mr. Quentain?" she asked, her voice betraying the fear which was welling up in her.

"He is not here."

"He was supposed to be!" she exclaimed.

"Really?" the Major said, seeming amused.

"What kind of game are you trying to play?" she demanded in a frightened voice.

"I'm here to meet you," he said.

Terror shadowing her lovely face, she said, "I have no desire to meet you. This is some sort of trick!"

She turned to run out of the vault but before she could do so the Major seized her roughly and threw her down on the hard earthen floor of this resting place for the dead. She cried out as she fell and hit the ground with her shoulder which immediately began to hurt. Before she could scramble to her feet the Major had rushed by her and escaped from the vault. She saw him make his exit and then the iron doors slammed shut to her utter dismay! She was a prisoner in the damp, dark vault!

With a groan she clutched her aching shoulder with one hand and staggered forward. She stumbled once and went on until she reached the cold metal of the vault doors. She vainly tried to push one of them open without any results. The doors had clearly been bolted in place and there was no hope of her escaping.

She leaned weakly against the metal doors and began to sob. She was terrified to be a captive in this foul, dark place and she tried to think what mistake she had made. She realized that it could be traced back to her accepting the undertaker as authentic and as being sent to her by Jeremy.

Now she knew she should have suspected him. But all the facts had suggested that he was genuine enough. Jeremy had not returned and no one had come with the remains of her brother. She knew something must have happened. The story offered her by the bogus undertaker had appeared a logical answer. Now she recalled his odd appearance and the heavy smell of whiskey on his breath.

What a fool she had been! She fought to halt her sobbing and gazed into the darkness of the huge vault, debating whether there might be some means of escaping at the other end of it. But she suspected the chances would be slim as that end of the vault was sure to be deep underground.

All at once she thought she heard sounds from outside. The vague echoes of voices which she could not make out and sounds of movement. This at once renewed her hope of getting free of the fetid vault and she began to pound on the rusty iron doors and scream.

"Help me! I'm a prisoner in here!" she cried out at the top of her lungs.

Then she heard a scraping noise as someone drew back the bolts on the doors and her heart gave a great leap of hope. She took a step back waiting to be rescued. The doors were suddenly thrown open and standing just outside was Carlos, holding a blazing torch, and beside him was the beautiful Contessa in a royal purple coat and velvet bonnet of the same hue. The Contessa offered her a cold, malevolent smile!

Chapter Eight

"You!" Adele cried out in despair.

"I thought you'd be glad to see me," the Contessa mocked her, the large green eyes glittering strangely in her lovely face. "I have come to rescue you!"

"I don't believe that!" she retorted.

The Contessa pursed her lips. "How skeptical you are! And I only want to be your friend!"

"You murdered my brother," Adele accused her.

"Not at all," the Contessa said with another mocking smile. "You have been getting your information from the wrong source."

"I think not," she said. She stepped out by the Contessa and went on, "Now if you will let me go!"

"I'm afraid that is impossible," the beautiful Contessa said. "Not in your present mood!"

Major Merrithew stepped out from the shadows and joined them. He said, "We shouldn't lose any time!"

"You are right, Major," the Contessa said, turning those odd eyes on her henchman. "You take Miss Foster with you. Carlos and I will join you later."

Adele made an effort to escape but the Major was too quick for her and caught her in his arms. She struggled to break his hold on her, "Let me go!" she cried.

"No chance of that!" he said, breathing heavily from the effort of struggling with her. "You're coming along with me, my girl!"

She cried out again but it was no use. There was no one to hear her. She heard the Contessa's mocking laughter following her as the Major trundled her off to a waiting cab.

The man who had posed as the undertaker was the driver of the cab. He helped the Major shove her inside and then jumped up to the driver's seat and started the vehicle on its way without waiting for directions. Evidently he knew exactly where this evil gang were taking her.

In the cab she turned angrily on the Major. "You will regret your share in this! Jeremy Quentain will see to that!"

The Major's coarse, bloated face showed an expression of derision in the rocking cab. He said, "The name of Jeremy Quentain does not scare me!"

"You will find him someone to be reckoned with," she told him.

He chuckled. "Do you think he can harm the Contessa? If you do, you're wrong!"

"Jeremy has promised to defend me," she said. "And he will!"

"We'll see about that," the man beside her said.

"Why are you doing this?" she demanded.

"The Contessa thinks you may try to interfere with her plans," was his reply as the cab was driven on.

"Where are we going?"

"London town!" The Major mocked her. "It's a large city, you know, with many a dark hole to hide someone away. Let us say we are contributing to your education!"

"Jeremy will punish you for this!" It sounded futile and stupid, even to her, but it was all she could think of to say.

The Major paid no heed to this but continued to keep a sharp eye on her. She thought about trying to jump out of the moving vehicle and escape but knew the chances were against her being successful.

After what seemed an endless time the vehicle came to a halt. Since the blinds were drawn down she could not tell where they had passed through. The Major grasped her arm in an iron grip and warned her, "Any nasty goings-on by you will only end in your getting hurt!"

She made no reply since she knew it was all too likely to be true. Tears of humiliation filled her eyes as the Major and the driver got her down from the cab and she found herself in a dark, narrow street.

"You won't need me any longer?" the driver suggested.

"No. You can go back," the Major said. "We'll walk the rest of the way."

The driver got up onto the carriage and started the single gray horse on its way as the Major dragged her across the dark, filthy street into an equally dark alley. He seemed to know exactly where he was going since he did not hesitate on his course.

She could hear drunken laughter somewhere close at hand as they emerged into a bleak courtyard. The fog was not so thick here and she could see the ancient tenements around the court stretching up to the sky.

A dog barked and she saw a mangy black and white fox terrier come racing up to them. The Major let out an oath and kicked at it. The dog yelped and ran off again with its tail between its legs.

The Major took her down another dark alley which stank and again she heard the sounds of voices, this time a couple cursing at each other in a fearsome manner. The Major continued on with his prisoner.

Now they came out in another court and he led her to an opening in which there had been a door, now torn away. She had heard that the poor in these wretched districts often removed doors in this manner for wood to burn to keep from freezing. The end result was that their houses were colder than ever with the doors gone. Misery begat misery!

A youthful ruffian was leaning against the building by the opening. She realized that he must be a sort of lookout. He at once recognized the Major and nodded to him without moving or saying a word. She looked into the face of the ruffian and saw the stubble of beard on his chin and the look of grim amusement on his coarse features. She could expect no help from that source, she decided.

Inside the foul-smelling house the Major shunted her down a dark passage that ended at a door with a light showing under it. He swung open the door and went inside with her. She was at once aware of some new odor in the air. A kind of sickly, sweet smell. And she saw that she was in a square-shaped room of some size with a rough bunk built against one wall. On the bunk sat a weird, bald man in a kind of flowing robe. He was curled up on the bunk with a candle lit near him and in his hand he held a long-stemmed clay pipe. The stem of the pipe was perhaps a foot and a half in length. And it was from this pipe that the odd, sweet-smelling smoke came.

The figure on the bench smiled at them in a dazed fashion and said, "Who is the girl, Major?"

"I found her on the streets," the Major said curtly. "The Contessa is interested in her."

"Take her in back," the man on the bunk ordered in a dreamy voice and sat back to puff on the long-stemmed pipe.

Only then did she realize that the smell which she had noticed was opium. And that the man on the bunk was a drug addict. Her horror was increased by the knowledge that she was going to be held captive in an opium den! The Major pushed her into a back room lit by one glittering candle on a bare, wooden table and forcibly sat her down on a wooden bench by the table.

Standing above her, he said, "Stay here and make no trouble and you won't be hurt!"

"Let me go!" she pleaded. "I can pay you well!"

The Major laughed hoarsely. "Your

money doesn't interest me." And he turned and marched out of the room.

She sat there miserably on the bench in the small, badly lighted room, wondering what might happen next. She began to have a conviction that she'd not escape this place alive. The Contessa wanted her out of the way so there would be no problems in taking over the estate. With John dead she was the only obstacle. So the evil gang was eliminating her from the scene.

Now she heard the Major talking with someone in the other room. He was keeping his voice purposely low so she could not tell what he was saying. Then she heard somebody else entering the outer room. There seemed to be two newcomers, a man and an old woman. The man had a sly, insinuating way of talking and the old woman was loud and vulgar in manner.

The man addressed himself to the Major, asking him, "What about this girl you have here?"

"She's a beauty," the Major said. "The Contessa wants her out of the country. The Contessa says she's not to be heard of again, ever!"

The old woman gave a burst of laughter. "Trust the tender thing to us and you needn't worry about that!"

The Major said, "That is why I sent for you. The word is out that Fancy Frank and Mother Green are always in the market for young women."

"We can always find a place for someone with good looks," the man with the oily voice said. "But don't try to foist any street bawd off on us. We're looking for fresh material!"

"That's what I have to offer," the Major said. "This is a fine young lady!"

The old woman shrieked with laughter again. "The demand for fine young ladies never dwindles!"

The conversation induced new terror in Adele. There could be no doubt that the Major had contacted some enterprising firm of white-slavers and he was now casually making a bargain with them to take her off his hands. The hopelessness of her plight brought her close to fainting and she leaned on the bare table for support and listened.

"What do you expect?" the man with the oily voice asked.

"Not a sovereign," the Major said. "We just want this young woman out of the way and your assurance that she'll never get back to London."

"We can promise that," the old crone shrilled. "None of them ever come back.

Some of them die and some move on. But they never come back! We can't afford to let them!"

The oily-voiced male said, "She will be sent directly to Belgium. From there she'll be shipped to Marseilles after a suitable time. The next stop is a port in Italy. If she survives that she goes to Morocco!"

"Maybe she should be sent to Morocco first," the old hag suggested. "She'd fetch a fine price from one of those sheiks!"

"We have to do it the usual way," the oily-voiced one said firmly. "Too risky otherwise. Mind you, if she isn't attractive the deal is off!"

"I'm not afraid of that," the Major said. "Go in and take a look at her for yourself."

"I will," the oily-voiced one assured him. "And another thing. There won't be any row about this! The Scorpion backs our operation and he doesn't like any trouble."

The Major said, "The Scorpion has no need to worry. He and the Contessa are old friends. She called on you two because he had recommended you."

"I wondered why you chose us," the old crone said. "Is she apt to give us any trouble?"

The oily-voiced man said, "We'll bind her wrists and gag her mouth. There's not much she can do beyond kick a little and we can take care of that!"

"Better get her and leave," the Major said. "How long will she be kept in London?"

"She'll leave for Belgium on the first sailing for Ostend in the morning. We'll give her a drop of the right stuff and she'll march on board like the little lady she is without having any idea what is going on."

"Oh, we know what we're about!" the old woman hooted.

"Very good," the Major said, sounding slightly disgusted. "I say get under way at once."

"Come in and help me bind and gag her," the oily-voiced one said.

The Major came back into the room with the man known as Fancy Frank. She could see how he managed to get his name. He wore loud plaid trousers and a fancy yellow jacket and a red cravat. His hat was yellow with a red band and he had a light blond Vandyke beard and mustache. He leered at Adele in a manner which made her blood run cold.

He said, "I wouldn't mind keeping this filly for my own stable."

The Major gave him a reproving glance. "That's out! You have to assure me she goes to Belgium or the deal is off."

The oily-voiced man looked sad. "That's the final word?"

"The Contessa said Belgium."

"Then Belgium it will be," Fancy Frank said with a sigh. "But I call it a waste. I promise you I do!"

Adele had risen and was standing with her back pressed against the far wall of the room. The blond, bearded Fancy Frank took a length of cord from his pocket and held it out in a businesslike fashion.

"Now, my dear," he said in a wheedling tone. "Just a bit of this around your wrists. You be nice to Frank and he'll be nice to you!"

"No!" she sobbed, backing into the corner which was as far as she could go.

The Major's coarse face showed amusement. "You better go along with what he says," he warned her. "You're not going to escape no matter what!"

"That's right, my dear," Fancy Frank said moving in on her so that she could smell the cologne with which he'd doused himself.

"Please! Let me go! I'll pay you anything!" she begged.

Fancy Frank's answer was to quickly grasp her wrists and in a deft movement wrap the cord around them and draw it cruelly tight. She cried out in pain and he laughed.

"Don't move your wrists and it won't hurt so, my dear," he told her.

"You have a way with women!" the Major said encouragingly.

"Tricks of the trade," Fancy Frank gloated. "I know them all."

"You and Mother Green must have given a lot of girls that Belgian holiday," the Major chuckled.

"We have a steady trade," Fancy Frank said, taking a colored bandana from a rear pocket and leering at her again. "This is my own clean handkerchief, my dear. You mustn't mind it. Just a small precaution so you won't shout and make us have to damage you. I dislike damaging fine goods!"

"No!" she cried again and twisted her head.

But she wasn't quick enough to avoid his expert moves. In a matter of seconds he had her gagged with the handkerchief and it tied tightly at the back of her neck. Now she was helpless except for being able to walk.

Fancy Frank gave her another of his nasty smiles. "Who knows how friendly we'll get along the way?"

The Major spoke up. "I don't care about that just as long as she gets to Belgium in the morning!"

"She will, I promise," the dapper desperado said. And he took her by the arm and dragged her out of the room with him.

Outside, the old woman known as Mother Green was seated with the opium smoker. She had a black shawl drawn over her head and held tightly about her face. But the eyes which stared out from the shadows of the shawl were mean and terrifying.

She croaked, "Call that one a beauty! I don't see it! I had twice her looks when I was her age!"

"That was a long while ago, Mother," the Major guffawed. "Before you did your turn on the streets."

"I was never on the streets," Mother Green said with anger. "I was a kept beauty. I had me own house until the old Duke died!"

Fancy Frank gave her an impatient look. "We haven't time to hear about the Duke and you again, Mother. Time we were on our way. Mustn't keep this young woman waiting."

Mother Green hooted with laughter again. "Not for what she has in store!"

The weird-looking drug addict put aside his pipe for a moment and gazing up at the Major said, "You mustn't forget my payment, Major!"

The Major said, "No." And he rummaged in his pocket and then tossed two gold sovereigns contemptuously onto the bunk. "That will help your dreams!"

The drug addict slowly reached out and clasped the gold pieces in his hand. "Beautiful!" he whispered. "Thank you, Major." And he bowed to him.

Fancy Frank pushed her on ahead and said in her ear, "I can be good to you or I can be cruel. You're the one to decide. Give me no trouble and it will be all right."

She allowed herself to be taken out into the dark courtyard again where the bully still remained on guard. Fancy Frank and Mother Green took hold of an arm on either side and propelled her along.

Mother Green asked, "Will the cab be there for us?"

"I told him to wait," her partner said.

"That doesn't mean he'll be there," the old woman grumbled. "He's been drinking a lot lately. Not dependable."

"If he isn't we'll have to hail a cab," Fancy Frank said.

"How will we explain her?" the old woman wanted to know.

The oily-voiced man said, "Tie your shawl over her head so that it will hide most of the gag. Chances are her hands won't be noticed."

Adele listened with mounting fear, knowing that what he said was all too true. Most people would not be interested enough to give her a second glance on this dark night. They would be able to take her bound and gagged through the streets without anyone really noticing.

It seemed that the Contessa had won. Nothing that Jeremy could do would matter now. Adele felt she was doomed to be shipped to Belgium in a drugged state and consigned to a fate which would remove her from the world she had known. No doubt drugs would continue to be used on her until she wound up a battered, mindless wreck in some foreign brothel. It was typical of the Contessa that she had arranged a fate for her more diabolical than mere death!

The two dragged her along a dark passage and out into a narrow street. And there the carriage was waiting. They shoved her inside and Mother Green sat next to her to guard her while the man gave the driver his instructions. A moment later Fancy Frank had taken a seat opposite Adele and the carriage was rumbling on its way.

Adele closed her eyes and prayed silently. It seemed that she was now beyond help. Within a few hours she would no longer be in England. The two evil partners would be able to do with her what they liked.

"You are very resigned to your fate, my dear," Fancy Frank said in his oily voice. "And that shows your intelligence."

The old woman beside her laughed shrilly. "You have an eye on her for yourself! I know!"

"It is true I do fancy Miss Foster," Frank said. "Would you be kind enough to remove her gag, Mother Green? It can do no harm to allow her to talk now."

"All right, my pretty," the old hag croaked, and she turned and busied herself unfastening the gag. Within a moment the restraining handkerchief had been removed from Adele's mouth.

"That is much better. Now I can enjoy your lovely face," Fancy Frank said with a smile.

"If you don't let me go I'll kill myself the first chance I have," were Adele's first bitter words.

The old woman hooted. "You'll not get the chance, dearie!"

Fancy Frank smiled at Adele and then did a most remarkable thing. Reaching up, he removed his top hat and the blond wig under it. Then he deftly stripped the mustache and Vandyke beard from his face to reveal the ascetic features of Jeremy Quentain.

In his own voice, Jeremy said, "The charade has gone on long enough."

Adele couldn't believe her eyes. "You!" she gasped.

"That is right," Jeremy said with a melancholy smile. "Sorry to give you such a bad time but it was the only way we could save you."

"That's right," the crone beside her said. And she turned to see that Mother Green had removed her shawl to reveal the familiar sunken face of old Meg.

"I should have known you!" Adele said. "But you hid your face and changed your voice."

"Had to, dearie," Meg said with a shrill laugh. "We took the places of those other two the Major was expecting. Lucky he didn't know what they looked like."

Jeremy leaned over and began carefully untying Adele's wrists. "After we learned that you were captured by the Contessa we went to some lengths to discover what she had in mind for you. It was then we heard that she planned to deliver you into the hands of two well-known white-slavers."

Old Meg chuckled. "So Jeremy had a couple of his friends call on them and see that they were trussed up so they couldn't make their visit to get you. And we took their places."

Adele shook her head in wonder. "You

certainly convinced me. I was sure I would never see England again!"

"You wouldn't have if those two had taken you over," Jeremy assured her solemnly. "How do your wrists feel?"

She rubbed them. "They'll be all right."

He said, "We're on our way to your place."

Adele sat back against the carriage seat. "I still can't believe it. You were both so different and convincing."

"Our lives wouldn't have been worth a farthing if they had gotten on to us," old Meg assured her with a serious look on her wizened face.

"I can believe that," she said.

"No matter," Jeremy said. "We managed to get you out of that trap."

"I wouldn't have gone to St. Dunstan's cemetery with that man if he hadn't said he was taking me to you," she told Jeremy.

The tall, dark man nodded. "I guessed they had played some game like that."

"I didn't know what had happened," she said. "You hadn't returned and the body of my brother hadn't been brought to the house as you said it would."

"That's another story," Jeremy said grimly. "I'll tell you about it when we arrive at your house."

They drove on and came to the more fashionable section of the city. Old Meg expressed a desire to be left off at a certain corner.

She explained, "I have my street to ply. People expect to see me. Old Meg, the beggar, has more friends than you'd guess."

"I'm sure you do," Adele said. "But after what you have done for me tonight there's no need for you to beg on the streets for a living. I'll give you a room and board and a position in my house."

Old Meg hooted with laughter. "That's generous of you, dearie! It truly is! But old Meg likes to beg. I enjoy the streets. It's the way I want to live."

Jeremy nodded for Adele's benefit. "You may find that hard to believe," he said. "But it is true. All Meg's friends are beggars like herself. It's a big fraternity and she'd be lost away from it."

So they dropped the old woman off at the corner of the street where she plied her beggar's trade. As the carriage drove on the ancient one stood highlighted under the gas lamp.

Adele turned to Jeremy and said, "I'd like to do something for her. She's a fine old woman."

"Knowing that you appreciate her is payment enough for Meg," Jeremy said. "She hates the evil members of the underworld though she is an underworld character herself. And it makes her feel good to fight them occasionally."

"You were both wonderful," she said.

"I also am interested in paying a debt," Jeremy reminded her.

At last they reached Adele's mansion and got out of the cab. There was still a thick fog but it was not as cold as it had been. With Jeremy at her side, Adele found the dark London night a lot less menacing.

When they went inside Marlow greeted them with a look of amazement. It was plain that the wild, yellow outfit which Jeremy had worn in the role of Fancy Frank was making a poor impression on the staid old hunchback.

He at once told Adele, "Your brother's body did not arrive."

"Thank you, Marlow," she said.

"Is there anything I can get you, Miss?" the old man wanted to know.

"No, thank you," she said. "I'm sure we can manage nicely on our own. You go to bed — you look very tired."

"Very good, Miss," Marlow said with gratitude. "I've been up all the night worrying about you."

She smiled thinly. "And now you see how needless that worry was."

"Yes, Miss," the old man said before leaving them.

She turned to face Jeremy. "Now what about my brother?"

He said, "Give me a moment. I feel ridiculous in this attire."

"Some of John's clothes are still here. You appear to be about the same size. Why not put one of his suits on?"

"Would you mind? I'm sure to be a laughing stock in this silly coat and trousers."

"I agree," she said. "Do go upstairs and change."

He did, and when he came down in the conservative brown suit he had borrowed from John's wardrobe he looked much more like the real Jeremy Quentain.

Adele greeted him by saying, "Now I feel it is truly you."

"I do feel better," he agreed wryly. "But the other costume was necessary for the part I was playing."

"You did it so superbly!" she enthused.

"I wasn't all that good," he said, with a suitable modesty.

"But you were and so was Meg," she said. "I shall never forget it. You had me terrified."

Jeremy nodded. "And now that you are safely back here I must tell you why I was delayed."

"Please do," she said as they stood facing each other in the drawing room.

He said, "Prepare yourself for a shock."

"What?"

"John's body is missing."

"Missing?"

"Stolen would be a better term," he said.

"Please tell me all," she begged him, sinking into a nearby chair.

His expression was stern. "When I left here I went directly to the undertaker's."

"And?"

"I found him recovering from being attacked and a chloroform rag being applied to his mouth and nose. The poor fellow was still in a dazed condition and your brother's body was gone."

She stared at him in dismay. "Why?"

His eyes met hers. "Can't you guess?"

"Because he was not truly dead?"

"He was dead in a sense," Jeremy said. "But as the victim of a vampire the curse has been passed on to him. John is now one of the living dead!"

"I was afraid of that," she agreed in a hushed tone.

"The Contessa wished him dead so that

she could inherit his estate but she also wanted him under her control as a vampire so she would have a new servant to do her bidding."

"So she had her evil associates steal his body?"

"Yes. Had she allowed it to be buried she would have had to steal it from his grave. This way was easier."

"And that explains the delay."

"Yes. I meant to get in touch with you but first I wanted to try and find the body. I failed in that and used far too much time. I fear that John is at large somewhere in London now, one of the vampire crew of whom the Contessa is the mistress."

"And while you were busy searching for John the Contessa came up with a plot to abduct me. She sent that fake undertaker here."

Jeremy nodded. "When I returned and found that you had gone with the supposed undertaker I knew exactly what had happened but I didn't know what to do about it."

"So?"

"I turned to my underworld associates and had them try to find out what was going on. I soon received word that the Contessa was taking you to that opium den near the docks and planning to turn you over to Fancy Frank and his partner."

"Then you had those two tied up while you and Meg took on their roles," she said.

"Fortunately we succeeded. Otherwise it could have gone badly for you."

"You don't need to tell me that," she said.

Jeremy sighed. "I hate to say this. But I think the best move on your part would be to leave London."

"With my brother the victim of this curse?"

"That can't be helped," the tall, handsome man said curtly. "When the Contessa finds she has been tricked she will be in a rage. It is hard to tell what she will do next."

Adele said, "I'm sure you are equal to her."

"Don't be too sure," Jeremy said gravely.

"I want my brother's unhappy spirit set at rest before I consider leaving here," she told him. "You must help me in that. A stake through his heart, or whatever is necessary, but he must be sent to a peaceful grave."

"He cannot be restored to life," Jeremy Quentain admitted. "And at present he is not truly dead. I can understand your feelings but it will take time to deal with him. And during that time you could come to harm."

"I cannot leave," she said stubbornly. "There is the matter of the estate and fighting the Contessa so that she cannot gain the share John left her."

"You are prepared to oppose her?"

"I must."

He sighed. "Then I shall stand by you. I promised that I would. But I must let you know the sort of uneven struggle this is apt to be."

"Please do."

"To begin with the Contessa is merely a puppet of the archcriminal known as the Scorpion. She is doing his bidding. And I hope to learn his identity and get at him through her. But that is my private battle."

"Because of what he had done to your wife?"

"Yes," Jeremy Quentain said, his face grim. "Because he had her murdered. I shall never rest until she is avenged."

"I do not blame you," she said quietly.

Jeremy said, "To return to the Contessa. The man employed by her and known as Major Merrithew is a living person the same as you and I. And so is Carlos. But all the others, and there are at least a half-dozen, including the Contessa, are of the living dead."

Chapter Nine

"I knew she must be a vampire," Adele exclaimed. "I could tell by the way she behaved in the cemetery last night. She was terribly strange and there was something about her eyes, a cruel glitter, that wasn't normal."

"If she had touched you her hand would have been as cold and clammy as the grave," Jeremy assured her.

"I'm sure she sleeps in a coffin in that house."

"My information indicates that. Each dawn she returns to the coffin and each twilight she rises to lead her gruesome company at the Scorpion's bidding."

She frowned. "Have you any idea who this Scorpion is?"

"I know certain things concerning him," Jeremy told her. "I have been led to believe he is an Englishman and that much of the time he lives in London."

"Is that all you know?"

"He is fiendishly clever and madly greedy," Jeremy went on. "He has an underworld army reaping him an evil profit. But he never has enough money or power. In the end that will be his downfall."

"And you are waiting for that time."

"I am," Jeremy agreed. "Gradually I am gaining much of the underworld on my side. My converts are the lesser figures of the dark world, those who commit the more harmless crimes, if a crime of any sort may be termed harmless. My people are beggars, petty thieves, prostitutes and confidence men."

"You draw the line at the violent."

"There are no murderers among them," he said solemnly. "They are the Scorpion's crew. I want no part of them."

"How did the Contessa come under his power?" she asked.

Jeremy began pacing back and forth restlessly as he talked. "She was living in Paris and tired of it. There she met Major Merrithew, who was on the Continent on an errand for the Scorpion. The Major found out the Contessa's secret and agreed to bring her to London for a price."

"And the price was?"

"That she become the servant of the Scorpion."

"She agreed?"

"Yes. But she insisted that Carlos also

come along. He has been her lover for years although he is a normal human being."

"So the Major spirited them across the channel to London."

Jeremy nodded. "Yes. The Contessa came over on the day boat in her coffin. By this time the Scorpion knew her history."

"What is her history?"

Jeremy halted and gave Adele a grim look. "For one thing she has been dead for fifty-two years."

"Fifty-two years!" Adele gasped.

"Yes. She was attacked and killed by a vampire in London when she was only twenty-four. The vampire who took her life was an Italian count by the name of Luigi Fillipio."

"And that is how she became known as a contessa?"

"Yes. Her real name is Elsie Perrin. She was a Cockney girl who became a prostitute and was set up in style by a titled man of wealth. He hired tutors to make her a lady and they did very well. But then the Count came along and became fascinated by her."

"Had she any knowledge that he was a vampire?"

"Apparently not," Jeremy said. "He wooed her in the absence of her regular lover and then gave her the fatal bite on the throat which took her life and made her his companion among the living dead forever!"

"Is the Count still active as a vampire?" she asked.

"Some say yes and some say no."

"What do you think?"

"I have heard one story," Jeremy said. "The party claimed that the Contessa never forgave Count Luigi for making her a vampire. And when Carlos came along and fell in love with her she enticed him to seek out the Count in his coffin during the daytime and drive a stake through his heart. This is the accepted way of causing a vampire to really die."

"It sounds a likely story," she said.

"I agree," Jeremy went on. "At any rate I have not heard that the Count is in London now. But the Contessa is and she has become one of the Scorpion's most productive criminals."

Adele said, "If she were alive she would be more than seventy-six years old and yet in her vampire state she remains a beauty of twenty-four."

"Yes," Jeremy said. "Strange that your brother should have fallen in love with her. It would have been different if he had guessed the truth."

"He could never dream of anything like that," she said.

"And now he is one of them," Jeremy said.

"So he must be sought out and destroyed," she said in a taut voice.

"It is a hard decision for you."

"I know it must be."

Jeremy came and placed a hand on her shoulder. He said, "The thing I most admire about you is your courage."

"I'm afraid I didn't show much of it when you took me captive as Fancy Frank," she said wryly.

"You had no opportunity then," he said. "You did the wise thing in accepting a fate you couldn't change."

She closed her eyes with a pained look on her lovely face. "Thinking about it now it seems like a nightmare."

"Regard it as that."

"I have been so stupid," she said.

"You can't be expected to match their criminal minds," was his reply. He gave her one of his piercing glances. "You are determined to remain in London. You will not leave this business to me alone?"

"I can't," she said. "I must stay for John's sake."

"Then we must be doubly careful from now on," Jeremy warned her. "The

Contessa will be ruthless in her desire for revenge."

"I'm sure of that," she said.

"I'm going to make a request of you," Jeremy said.

"Anything."

"Don't agree so quickly," he said. "You don't know what my request is."

"It doesn't matter."

"Maybe you will change your mind when I tell you," Jeremy said.

"What is it?"

"I want your permission to live in this house with you until all this is settled."

Her eyes widened. "You want to live here?"

"Yes."

"Of course," she exclaimed. "I'd be delighted to have you here. I'll feel that much safer."

"I can watch over you better in that way," he explained.

"I'm thankful that you've made the offer."

The handsome man said, "I wasn't sure how you'd feel about it."

"Now you know."

"Then I shall go to my cottage and get a few things," he told her. "After which I'll return here."

She got up. "I know your living here will

make all the difference. Much of my fear has vanished already."

"Don't become careless," he cautioned her.

"No," she said. "I mustn't do that."

"I'll be on my way," he said. "I don't wish to be too late returning."

She walked with him to the door. "Do be careful," she said. "Their rage is going to be chiefly directed at you."

"I'm used to that," he said with a wry smile. "And I have a number of friends to help me." With that he kissed her tenderly on the forehead and told her, "Give Marlow word that I'm returning and you go to bed. You look very tired."

"I will," she said.

After she'd seen him out she summoned Marlow and informed him of the fact that Jeremy Quentain would be living with them for a while.

"It is a temporary measure until the evil people who brought on my brother's death are punished," she said.

Marlow looked confused. "But what about Mr. John? Where is his body?"

"It was stolen," she told the hunchback servant. "Don't ask me why. It is all very mixed up."

"Yes, Miss," the old man said. And then,

as if remembering, he added, "By the way, Miss, young Mr. King called here tonight to pay his respects."

"Oh!"

"I told him you had gone out and it appeared to bother him. But he seemed less concerned when I said that you had gone with the undertaker to see Mr. Quentain."

"What did he say?"

"He asked that you be told he'd called and said he would like to see you. He spoke of being in his office tomorrow morning if you had the time to call on him there."

"Thank you, Marlow," she said. "I'll keep that in mind."

"Yes, Miss," the old servant said and went on his way.

She was pleased to learn that Richard King had come as he'd promised. And she made up her mind to try and visit him at his office. She wanted to tell him of the latest happenings and also that Jeremy Quentain had decided to live in the old mansion with her until something was done about the Contessa.

Slowly mounting the stairs she went up to her bedroom. Her bed was turned down and a lighted lamp had been set out on the dresser. She went to the window and saw that it was still foggy out. And her mind turned to the Contessa. The news which Jeremy had offered her had been surprising. She would never have guessed that the vampire Contessa had such humble English origins or that she was almost three-quarters of a century old by regular standards.

It had been a trying day and a worse evening. She was thoroughly exhausted and the prospect of bed and a sound sleep seemed more important than anything else. Jeremy had said not to wait up for him and there seemed no reason why she should. Marlow would let him in when he returned.

As she lay waiting for sleep she thought about Jeremy and of Richard King. Both men appealed to her strongly. Perhaps she felt more confidence in Jeremy but she could not overlook the fact that Richard was more pleasant. Jeremy was still under the shadow of his wife's murder and she worried that he might never emerge from it. It had radically changed his thinking.

Perhaps she should be grateful for that. Otherwise he would never have been willing to enlist on her side in the battle with the Contessa. But if she were to make a choice of one of the two men as a husband she would be hard pressed to decide which it would be. These random thoughts filled her mind as she sought sleep. Finally it came.

She awoke with a start to the darkness of her room. She had been having a horrible dream in which she'd been pursued by the Major and Carlos. Now that she was awake the nightmare was still prominent in her mind. She had raced through endless dark streets to escape the two and in the end they had caught her. She'd wakened herself as she cried out in her nightmare.

Staring into the shadows she attempted to dispel the fear which she still felt. But the events of the evening plus her dream were too great for her to throw off. She was frightened and she couldn't help it. She knew it must be long after midnight and she wondered if Jeremy had returned. It was the time of night for ghosts to prowl!

The stillness of her room seemed strange in itself. It was almost too still. Her fear began to increase and she stared into the darkness to the right and left, as if she were expecting some sinister development.

It was then that she heard a footstep in the corridor outside as if someone coming down the hall had halted out there and was listening at her door. Her first thought was that it might be Jeremy.

She called out, "Jeremy, is that you?"

There was no answer as she waited a little longer. She began to have all sorts of terrified thoughts. Perhaps it was the Contessa out there or one of her associates. And she feverishly reached for the crucifix which she had made it a habit to wear as protection against the vampire crew.

She gasped. For the crucifix was missing! Either she had lost it in the melee of the early evening when she'd been taken captive by the Major or it had been removed from her throat while she slept. She felt unprotected without it!

No sooner had she made this discovery than the door to her room began slowly to creak open. Frozen with fear and wide-eyed she stared at it. And there framed in the doorway was the ghostly figure of her brother, John. His face was pale and tense just as it had been when she'd seen him in the police station morgue. It was the eyes that were different. Now his eyes had taken on that same weird glitter she'd noticed in the green eyes of the Contessa. And his lips, which appeared to have thickened, twitched as he came directly to the foot of her bed.

She finally managed to whisper hoarsely, "Johnny!"

His weird eyes fixed on her as he said, "You have made a bad error."

"What do you mean?"

The ghostly figure intoned, "You must

not try to battle the Contessa. It is my wish that she have my share of all that we own."

"You can't mean that!" she protested, forgetting that she was talking to a dead man.

"I have come here to so inform you," her brother said.

"It's the Contessa! She has placed a spell on you!"

John showed no change of expression. "She has made me one of her own kind. I am happy to serve her."

"You are cursed!" Adele sobbed. "You have become one of the living dead! She did that to you!"

Her brother stretched out a hand to her across the shadows and invited her, "Why do you not join me?"

"No!" she cried, shrinking back against the pillows. "Don't come near me!"

He came around the side of the bed. "Do not think I will harm you. Let me touch my lips to your throat and you will enter this twilight world of bliss I know!"

"Johnny!" she screamed in fear as he drew back his lips to reveal the prominent white teeth beneath them and came close to her, ready to sink those teeth in her throat in the vampire manner.

She quickly swung out of the bed on the other side and raced for the door. Without turning back she knew the ghostly figure of her brother was pursuing her. She ran down the length of the corridor sobbing and trying to think of some way to escape!

The crucifix! If only she still had the crucifix she might have been able to keep him off with that. But the crucifix had vanished. This thought led to another one. There was a chapel in the old mansion, long unused. In earlier days a religious family had owned the property and had a private chapel for devotions. It was on the lower level and at the rear of the house. She vaguely recalled its altar and felt sure there was a crucifix on the wall above it.

Breathlessly reaching the landing at the rear of the house she turned for a brief moment to see the spectral figure of John come stalking down the dark hallway in pursuit of her. She screamed again and began racing down the stairs. She dare not stumble since he was so close to her that she could smell the fetid odor of death from him!

When she reached the lower hallway she made directly for the chapel and flung the door open. The large room with its altar and rows of pews smelled of dust and neglect. Sobbing she ran down the short aisle and clambered up on the altar. Then she began groping along the wall for the crucifix which she knew must be there.

Meanwhile the phantom figure of her brother had entered the chapel and was slowly coming down the aisle towards the altar. His pale face wore a chastened look in this holy place and he edged his way towards her in an almost frightened fashion.

"Come down from there!" he intoned.

"No!" she cried.

"I only want to help you," John said.

"Go away!" she implored him as she still feverishly sought for the crucifix.

"Come with me, Adele," her brother pleaded, now at the altar and ready to step up on it and attack her.

"No!" she told him as she felt her hands close on the crucifix. Frantically she lifted it from its place on the wall and turned holding it up so that it was between her and the vampire beast which her brother had become.

He raised a clawlike hand to protect himself and screamed, "Don't! Put it away!"

"Leave me!" she cried, brandishing the crucifix close to him.

He uttered a pained, moaning sound and staggered back in the shadows. A dreadful dissolution seemed to come over him and his mouth gaped open as his eyes filled with a horror such as she had never seen before. Then very swiftly he literally dissolved into the shadows. One moment he was there in the midst of his torment and the next he was gone!

The strain had been too much for her. With the crucifix still clutched in her hands she uttered a soft cry of despair and fell in a heap on the altar.

It was there that Jeremy and Marlow found her, Jeremy bending over her anxiously while Marlow stood by holding a candle. She opened her eyes and saw the two and gave a small moan of relief.

Jeremy said, "What happened? What brought you down here?"

She fixed her eyes on the handsome, weary face of Jeremy as she said, "It was John!"

"John?" Jeremy echoed her.

"Yes. He came to me in vampire form. I had no way to protect myself from him. My crucifix was gone."

Jeremy was staring at her in amazement. "So you came down here?"

"I remembered the chapel and the crucifix on the wall."

Jeremy said, "What then?"

"I was able to fend him off. He vanished. But it was too much. I fainted."

"Not much wonder," Jeremy said grimly. "Can you get to your feet?"

"I think so," she said. "There's really nothing wrong with me except fright."

Jeremy assisted her to her feet and then told Marlow, "Get your mistress some brandy."

"Yes, sir," the old hunchback said. And placing the candle holder with the lighted candle on the altar he hurried off on the errand.

Jeremy gave her a solemn look. "I couldn't have been gone long when this happened."

"No," she said. "I went to bed and it happened soon after."

"I came back and found the door to your bedroom open and you vanished," he said. "Marlow and I began a search of the house for you and found you here."

She gave him a troubled look. "It was John. I saw him clearly and he even talked to me. He is mad! He's become one of them! One of the living dead!"

"We'd already guessed that," Jeremy said with a sigh.

"He tried to attack me and have me become one of them as well; it was horrible!"

Jeremy gave her a warning glance. "You had best be prepared for it to happen again.

John, or the Contessa, or some one of them will undoubtedly try to destroy you."

"It's like some awful nightmare!" she said. "Bad enough to know John is dead but to have him like this!"

"He must be put at rest," Jeremy said. "But we can worry about that later."

Marlow returned with the brandy. And when she had sipped a glass of it Jeremy saw her safely to her room. "You'll not be bothered again tonight," he predicted. "And should you be I'll be close by in the room across the corridor."

"I don't think I'll sleep," she said.

He touched her arm in a gesture of comfort. "I'm sure you will. And to give you further assurance keep the crucifix by your bed."

"I will," she said. She still held the large wooden crucifix in her hands.

And so the eerie happenings of the night came to an end. She finally slept as Jeremy had predicted she would. And when she awoke it was morning and the fog had vanished. It was a day of sunshine and there was only the crucifix on her bedside table to remind her of the horror of the dark hours.

It was a pleasant experience to sit with Jeremy at the breakfast table. She told him that Richard King had come to see her on the previous night.

She explained, "He asked that I come by his office this morning."

"He doesn't know about your brother's fate yet," Jeremy said.

"No. Marlow told him I had gone to St. Dunstan's cemetery with the undertaker to meet you. That was what I had expected to do, not knowing the undertaker was an imposter leading me into a trap."

Jeremy paused over his coffee with a frown. "I intend to seek out a friendly inspector at Scotland Yard this morning and have him work on the theft of your brother's body."

"Is he apt to believe the story about the vampires?"

"Probably not," Jeremy said. "Yet I think I should do this. It may help us in other ways."

"You know best," she said.

"I'd like to get into that house during the day while the Contessa is sleeping in her coffin," the dark, handsome man said.

"That could be terribly dangerous," she suggested.

He nodded. "The house is barricaded like a fortress. But there is no fortress which can't be invaded. One has only to find the weak point and use the right method."

"You have the Major and Carlos to contend with. Neither of them are under the shadow of the vampire curse so they are bound to be alert during the daylight hours."

"True," Jeremy agreed.

"I don't know which I fear the most," she sighed.

"Carlos," Jeremy said promptly. "The Major is drunken and that makes him the easier of the two to dupe. Carlos is also terribly cruel."

"You say he destroyed the Count Fillipio?"

"After he became the Contessa's lover," Jeremy agreed. "Not that I consider the Count to have been any upright character. It was he who turned Elsie into the vampire Contessa. A nasty bit of handiwork if I may say so."

She gave him a direct look. "But in your mind the chief villain is still this person known as the Scorpion."

"He is the criminal mind who offers leadership to the others," Jeremy said.

"Then he is the important one to destroy."

"I know that, but the prospect is small. He is wary."

She said, "The Contessa wants this house. I expect we'll soon be hearing about that from her lawyers."

"You must fight her in the courts," Jeremy said. "At least until we manage to deal with her in some other fashion."

They finished breakfast and then Jeremy set out for Scotland Yard to discuss the disappearance of Adele's brother's body with his inspector friend. Adele went upstairs and dressed for her excursion into the city.

When she went downstairs she told Marlow where she was going and said, "I should be back for lunch."

The old servant asked, "Will Mr. Quentain be joining you?"

"I expect so," she said. "I really don't know."

"I shall prepare for him as well," Marlow said.

"That would be wise," she agreed. "And if anyone asks for me you can tell them I've gone to see Mr. King."

"Yes, Miss," the old man said.

The carriage was waiting for her and she gave the driver the address and stepped into it. The London streets were busy on this fine day and consequently the traffic was slow. A wagon and an omnibus were in collision at a corner of one of the most-traveled streets and there was a long wait and resulting confusion.

She watched out of the window of the carriage while the driver of the horse-drawn bus and the burly owner of the wagon threatened each other and called each other names. The crowd at the scene seemed to be thoroughly enjoying the near fist-fight. At the same time an enterprising vendor of hot periwinkles had set up a stand nearby and had begun vending his wares.

Finally two agitated and mustached Peelers arrived at the spot and began taking notes and clearing up the traffic snarl. After a wait of ten minutes more Adele's carriage again got underway.

When they reached the intersection of the street where Oglethorpe and Huestiss had their law offices she looked out and saw that this thoroughfare was also busy with traffic. So she leaned forward and told the driver, "Let me off at the corner. It will save me time."

"Yes, Miss," the coachman said.

She told him, "You may as well drive back. I'll find a cab to bring me home. It's too busy today for you to wait for me here."

"Very well, Miss," the coachman said.

She left him and made her way along the narrow sidewalk in the direction of the law office. As she neared the moment of seeing young Richard King again she felt her pulse quicken and knew a growing excitement.

His was the most important friendship she'd formed in London — that is, if you excluded Jeremy. And she had come to know the handsome, melancholy Jeremy through Richard King. She regarded Jeremy as her chief ally in combating the Contessa. But she felt differently about Richard. He was perhaps closer to her in a personal way.

She wondered what the young lawyer would think about Jeremy having moved into her house. He might think it strange, perhaps. Yet Richard knew of the danger in which she lived while she remained in London. Surely he would understand.

Mounting the steps of the ancient brick building she went directly to the door of the law offices, and after knocking gently, opened the door and stepped inside. She had expected to see the old clerk at his high desk. But the old man was not seated there on his tall stool to receive her in the usual fashion. The office was empty. She stood there hesitantly, thinking that the silence there was positively eerie!

Chapter Ten

The tension she felt made her want to cry out. Fear marked her lovely face as she gazed around her. The outer office was completely deserted.

Still standing there she called out, "Richard?"

There was no reply. She saw that the door to the inner office was standing a trifle ajar. It seemed odd to her that her call hadn't been answered. Surely Richard or his uncle ought to have been there even if the old clerk were out on an errand.

After waiting a moment she crossed over to the door and slowly drew it all the way open. She looked into the inner office and found it also empty. It simply didn't make sense. She turned to go back to the outer office and leave when she suddenly halted and stopped dead in her tracks.

Standing in the middle of the outer office and facing her was the sinister Carlos in his black cape and black homburg hat. The white-haired man offered her a malicious smile as he said in his slightly accented voice, "Are you so surprised to see me again, Miss Foster?"

Shocked, she said, "What are you doing here?"

"May I not also ask the same question?" he wanted to know.

Her fear increasing she demanded nervously, "Where is Richard King? What have you done with him?"

The black eyebrows of Carlos rose in pretended surprise. "Are you suggesting I may have done him harm?"

"I'm certain that you have," she said. "Tell me!"

"We haven't time to discuss that," Carlos told her with another of his mocking smiles. "I want you to come along with me."

"Never," she said, drawing back.

A cruel gleam showed in the white-haired man's eyes as he took a step towards her. "Let me warn you I am not the Major. You will not find me so easy to deal with!"

"Don't come near me!" she cried.

"Little fool!" he said with disgust and he quickly moved forward and seized her.

She struggled and cried out but it did no good. Within a matter of a moment he had her gagged and her hands tightly tied in front of her. Then with a smile he produced a veil and a small white shawl from a leather case which he'd been carrying.

"All the well-dressed young women wear veils," he said with evil amusement as he put this one over her face and drooped it about her bonnet. Then he hung the white shawl over her bound hands so it covered the binding. "And a shawl is often useful when the London weather is cool."

He then took her by the arm and warned her, "I have a knife concealed in my hand. Make any attempt to run off or attract attention and I swear I'll plunge it into you. I can do it and be off free before anyone realizes what has happened. Just remember that!"

She was filled with humiliation and despair. In seeking out Richard the last thing she'd expected was to walk into a trap. And yet she had. And to make things worse she was sure something horrible had happened to the young man who had been so kind to her. Jeremy had warned her that Carlos was the most dangerous one and it was proving to be all too true.

Once again she was a prisoner and this time Jeremy was not on hand to rescue her. She was alone and trapped. Carlos would show her small mercy.

"Now walk along with me like a demure

young lady," Carlos instructed her. "And remember, one false move, and you are dead!"

She knew that he meant what he said. There was no need for him to offer the threat again. And she also knew that, unlike the Major, this was a truly crafty foe. Sick with fear she let him lead her out of the office and into the street.

Major Merrithew was out there on the sidewalk with a carriage waiting for them. His bloated face showed a triumphant smile as he saw them. "Well, Miss Foster is giving us the honor of her company once again!" was his comment.

"She insisted," Carlos said grimly. "Do you not think the veil becomes her?"

"The ideal ornament," the Major said with a chuckle. And he assisted her up into the dark interior of the carriage. "You eluded us last night but now we can begin again."

She sank down on the hard seat as the others got in with her. The carriage started off and she forlornly realized that she was in their hands once again. All the efforts of the previous night had been in vain. They would have their way. And where were they taking her? Maybe to the boat leaving for Belgium. It might not be too late for that. They might be able to carry out their nefarious scheme exactly as they'd planned the previous night.

"Jeremy Quentain rescued you last night," Carlos said with a sneer. "But he won't be able to get you away from us this time."

"This time you will do as we wish," Major Merrithew said. "By the time they find you are missing it will be too late."

Adele bowed her head and the tears brimmed from her eyes and rolled down her cheeks. She was grateful for the veil which hid her misery from them. The carriage jolted over the rough streets, halting every so often for traffic until it finally came to a halt.

The two men trundled her out of the carriage and she saw that she was in an alley. Almost at once she recognized it as being the alley by the Contessa's house. It had been through that alley she had managed her escape with the help of old Meg. The mere remembrance of this escapade served to give her a touch of courage. If she'd managed it before she might again. But this time no one would know where she was.

The Major was ahead of her and Carlos. He halted and unlocked a padlock and opened a sturdy door which led to steps descending into darkness. He stood by while

Carlos roughly shoved her inside and down the dark steps. She almost lost her footing but he managed to save her. They reached the earthen floor of the cellar and walked a distance across it to another stairway.

They went up these stairs and she recognized that she was in the corridor of the ground floor of the house. She knew that all the lower floors were empty. The Major had rejoined her and Carlos and now the three of them climbed the several flights of stairs to the upper floor where the Contessa held court. She was taken into a small room and there Carlos untied her hands and took the gag from her mouth.

He told her, "If you behave, you'll have no trouble. If you don't, expect to be treated roughly."

"What do you think you've done to me already?" she asked.

"That's just a sample," the red-faced Major Merrithew said.

The two left her and she rubbed her wrists to bring back the circulation. Then she began to pace back and forth. The room in which they had placed her was bare of furniture and its single window was shuttered on the outside. A small amount of daylight filtered in around the shutters but otherwise the room was in shadow.

She began to review what had happened and try to think what had become of Richard King and the old clerk. She was sure they must have been attacked in some fashion by the two criminals who had brought her back to the Contessa's house. She fervently hoped that Richard might be safe. But she realized anything could have removed him from the scene. He might even be dead!

It was a frightening thought. And what of Jeremy? He would return to the house and find her missing. Then he would start a search which would first take him to Richard King's office. After that it would depend on what he found there or how much information Richard was able to give him. He would surely suspect the Contessa and her henchmen and sooner or later focus his attention on this house in which she was a prisoner.

But would he get to her in time? That was the important question. When twilight arrived and the Contessa rose from her coffin decisions would be made. Adele also feared that her brother might also be in the house with her. And if he came after her again as he had on the previous night she would be unable to elude him. It could be that her captors had changed their minds about her fate and were now planning to make her one of them — have her become another of the mindless vampire victims of the Contessa, ready to do her bidding.

It was not a pleasant thought to live with. The hours went by and though she had no idea of the passing time she knew that evening was at hand by the change in the light coming in around the shutters.

The door to the room was unlocked and Carlos appeared. He said, "Come along!" And he stood aside to let her walk out.

She obeyed him and found herself in another elegantly furnished room. The Major was seated in an easy chair nursing a drink in his hand and studying her, with satisfaction on his bloated face.

He said, "Time you had a spot of food and talked to the Contessa."

Carlos pointed to a table and chair. "There!" he said.

She saw, that there was food and drink on the small table. Because she was weak and thirsty she sat down and drank the hot tea offered and ate some of the meat set out on the plate.

When she finished Carlos told her, "Time for you to meet the Contessa again."

"I'd rather not," she told him quietly.

"Listen to her!" the Major laughed.

Carlos looked angry. "I don't think you have any choice, Miss Foster. I will ask you again to come with me. If you don't, I'll take you by force."

"Very well," she said with a dignity and calm which she did not feel. But she could not let them see her tremble and sob.

Carlos led her through an arched doorway and she found herself in the purple splendor of the satin-decorated bedroom of the Contessa. And there in the corner of the room in a coffin of polished mahogany lay the beautiful vampire. A lighted candle in a tall silver candlestick burned at the head of the coffin and another at the bottom of it. These candles provided the only light in the room.

She stood there staring down at the perfect face of the Contessa in the flickering glow of the candles. She appeared to be sleeping quietly and no one would have suspected that this beautiful creature was a denizen of the half-world capable of great evil.

Carlos stood beside Adele with a thoughtful look on his normally cruel face. He said, "Lovely, isn't she?"

"Yes," she said. "Too bad it is a mirage."

Carlos smiled evilly. "She is a genius, even as one of the living dead. I have dedicated my life to her."

She gave him a sharp glance. "Is it true that you drove a stake through the heart of her husband, the Count? That you destroyed him as a vampire."

The white-haired man showed surprise. "Who told you that?"

"Jeremy Quentain. And his information is usually correct."

"Too bad you won't ever see him again," Carlos sneered. And then his manner suddenly changed and in an awed voice, he said, "Watch! It is time!"

She stared at the body of the woman in the coffin and saw what he meant. The pale, motionless face had begun to show tiny signs of life. And as she watched she saw the mouth of the Contessa twitch and then a hand resting on her bosom opened and she appeared to be reaching up for something.

Now the Contessa's eyes opened and she stared blankly up for a moment or two before that weird glitter came to them and she abruptly sat up in her coffin.

Contessa Maria eyed Adele with pleasure. "So I have some unexpected company," she said.

"We captured her this morning in Richard King's office," Carlos informed her.

The Contessa said, "Help me down from here."

Carlos went to her and lifted her out of the coffin and onto the carpet. The Contessa stood there in an attractive, flimsy gown of pale blue and studied Adele again.

Carlos said, "We did nothing until we had a chance to talk with you."

The Contessa nodded in agreement. "That was wise." And to Adele, she said, "Do you still wish to oppose me, girl?"

"Yes," Adele said defiantly.

"You are being foolish," the Contessa told her. "I will win. I always do. Your brother is my slave now."

"I know," Adele said. "He came to me last night."

"He failed with you," the Contessa said harshly. "His orders were to attack you and make you one of us. But you frightened him off!"

"He is no longer my brother," Adele said. "You have made him a monster without a mind."

The Contessa showed a cold smile on her lovely face. "And that is precisely what I plan to do with you. Then I'll have no one to battle me about your estate."

"Jeremy Quentain will settle with you whatever you do to me," she said.

Carlos spoke up, "And what makes you

think we'll allow that Quentain to live? His end is in sight now."

"That's bravado!" she said. "I don't believe you."

"You will find out," the Contessa warned her.

Carlos said, "What now?"

The Contessa said, "She annoys me. Take her back to the room. Lock her up there until her brother wakes and joins us. Then we can let him deal with her as he tried to last night."

Carlos seized Adele by the arm again, saying, "You heard!"

He hurried her out of the room where the Contessa was standing and back to the empty room in which he'd first imprisoned her. As he shoved her in, he said with sarcasm, "When your brother arrives he'll be in to see you." And then he shut the door and locked it.

Now the room was in almost complete darkness. She stood there filled with terror. She knew what would happen. When John appeared in his vampire state they would send him in to attack her. She would have no hope of defending herself. In a few minutes it would be all over. She would become one of the vampires, lost to Richard, and lost to Jeremy! No hope!

She groped her way over to the window and tried it. But the sash wouldn't budge up and then there were the shutters outside. And even if the window were open she was stories high above the ground. The most she could hope for was the freedom to commit suicide. To hurl herself down to lie in a crumpled heap on the cobblestones far below. But better that than to become one of the living dead!

As she was deliberating about this she suddenly heard a kind of scratching noise from outside the window. She stared at it in disbelief, thinking that she must be imagining it. But the scratching continued. Now she gave her full attention to the window and after a moment the shutters were suddenly opened. Her surprise was so great she almost cried out. And as if this weren't enough she saw that a plank had been placed between the sill of a window in an adjoining house and the sill of her window!

A man in a black suit was kneeling on the plank and at the moment inserting something under the sash of her window. He pried at it and she was delighted to see the sash move. He then raised it up.

He motioned to her and in a whisper said, "Come with me!"

She stood by the window and saw how

narrow and thin the plank was, and the awesome drop to the ground below. She felt her head reel, and despite her urgent need to escape from the room, she knew that her fear of getting out on that plank was too great.

"No," she whispered. "I can't!"

"You must!" said the man outside. "I'm risking my life to save you!"

She stood hesitantly by the window. "I'll fall!"

"Risk it!" the man urged. "If you wait much longer your brother will be with you. Then there'll be no hope. Nothing that I or anyone else can do!"

"Who are you?"

"I'll tell you later," he said impatiently. "Come! I'll have to move back to the other window sill. The plank simply won't support both of us at once!"

"Take my hand!" she pleaded.

"As soon as you're part way over and I safely can," the man said. And he began backing across to the other building.

There was nothing she could do but begin the perilous journey across the plank. Biting her lip, she thrust herself out the window and slowly began creeping across the plank. She did not dare look below. The plank swayed a little and she curbed a scream as she had the sickly feeling she was about to fall.

"Quickly!" the man in the other building said hoarsely.

"I can't!" she moaned.

"Keep on!" he urged.

She stopped and felt she could not resume. But he kept urging her on and at last she began again. This time she came close enough that he could hold out his hand and clasp hers. Then she managed the rest of the way. She was shaking like a leaf as he helped her in through the window of the other room.

"You have great courage," he told her.

"I think I'm going to faint," she murmured.

His arm was supporting her. "Nonsense! You're only partly safe. I've got to get you out of here and back to your home before we can relax an instant."

She stared at him in the shadows. "Did Jeremy send you?"

"No," he said.

"He must have," she insisted. "It was always Jeremy and his helpers who rescued me before!"

"This time it isn't," the man said. "Come along with me. And no more talk about fainting unless you wish us both to be captured by that evil gang!"

He ushered her out of the room and down several flights of grimy stairs. When they came out onto the street he glanced from right to left to see there was no one about. Then he took her by the hand and hurried her down the narrow street. They fairly raced until they came to a busier section. And there he hailed a cab and gave the driver her home address.

As the cab jolted along through the night she studied him sitting in the seat across from her. He was not a large man and he was slight of build. She judged that he might be about fifty years old. His hair was iron gray and he had a neat mustache, also iron gray. His face was lined but she could see that at one time he might have been considered handsome.

Certainly his manners were excellent and he spoke in a cultured voice. And he was dressed richly though in a somber way. Surely this was a man of mystery. And she at once wondered if he might be the Scorpion. The criminal leader! But then she realized that the Contessa was an ally of the Scorpion, so he would not be likely to rescue someone she was holding prisoner.

Again she asked, "Who are you?"

"A friend," he said.

"That is not enough."

"It should be," the man said quietly.

"Why did you rescue me?"

"Because you deserved to be saved."

She was frustrated. "There has to be more than that," she insisted. "How did you know about me? That I was a captive? And why did you risk your life to save mine?"

The elegantly dressed man opposite her said, "Let us say I am not an admirer of the Contessa."

"Go on!"

"I make it my business to observe closely what she is doing. So I learned about your capture. Because I have a score to settle with her, I rescued you."

"Why?"

Hatred crossed the face which had once been handsome and he said, "Because the Contessa ruined my life!"

"How?"

"At the gambling tables. Don't you know that she operates one of the most successful gambling clubs in London?"

"No. It's the first I've heard about it," she admitted.

The man smiled bitterly. "The best people go there! It is a private club of course, and well hidden from the authorities. It occupies a fine house near Hyde Park and you can see the carriages of the rich and mighty drawing up there almost every night."

"The Contessa is the owner?"

"The Scorpion owns it and the Contessa operates it," the man across from her said. "It's very convenient to have one of the living dead as your manager. So difficult to get to them for any questioning in the daylight hours!" He laughed hoarsely.

She stared at him. "Then you know! I mean about her being a vampire!"

"I do now," he said. "I didn't then. Not when she and her gang swindled me for my fortune! I was one of the innocents who stood by the gaming tables every night thinking that one night I would find my luck changing."

"The games were crooked?"

"Rigged, every one of them!" the man said angrily. "And they still are. But no one thinks the lovely Contessa could be guilty of cheating. Would you believe it the Prince of Wales attends the casino? And there are those who say he once asked the Contessa to be one of his mistresses!"

"What if he knew about her?" she said in awe.

"I think His Royal Highness would be mightily upset," the man said. "And serve him right."

"So you plan revenge on the Contessa?"

"Yes."

"You should join forces with Jeremy

Quentain," she said. "He also has a score to settle with the Scorpion and the Contessa, not to mention the others. And so have I."

The man scowled. "I know about Quentain. I don't think he and I would get along."

"I think you would," she enthused. "I'd like you two to meet."

"Perhaps one day," he said.

"Because you rescued me he's bound to be grateful."

"I'm not interested in gratitude," the man across from her said.

"Whether you are or not, I can promise you I'm thankful and I'll always be."

The man gave her a hard stare. And after a moment of silence, he said, "I may ask you to do me a certain favor."

"Of course," she said. "What is it?"

"I can't tell you now," he said. "But I'll let you know later and I must insist that you carry out this favor on your own."

"I will," she promised.

"I want no one else to know about it, not even Jeremy Quentain," the man said.

"If that is what you want I cannot refuse," she said. "You saved my life tonight."

"You can pay me back in the way I have mentioned," the man told her in a business-like manner. "When the time comes I will call on you."

The more he talked, the more she was intrigued by him. She said, "I'll have to tell them I was rescued by someone."

"Just say it was by a man whom the Contessa ruined at the gaming tables."

"Very well," she said. "I don't suppose they'll be able to trace who you are from that."

"Hardly," he said with a grim smile. "She has ruined far too many. I'm merely one of a legion."

"And she is so beautiful."

"I was tricked by her beauty once," the man said. "Now I know better."

The cab halted and he helped her out to the sidewalk. He said, "I'll be waiting in the cab until I see you are safely inside. I don't want anyone in the house to see me."

She stared at him wistfully. "You are a man of mystery!"

He nodded. "For the time being I have to be."

"But I will hear from you later? When you come for the favor?"

"Yes," he said. "I will come back to you for that. I promise."

He got back in the cab and waved to her as she turned and mounted the steps of the old mansion. She knocked on the door and when Marlow opened it his wizened old face was a mask of shock.

"Miss Foster!" he exclaimed in his old man's voice. "You are back!"

"Yes," she said, with a pathetic attempt at a smile. "Don't you think it about time?"

"They'll be glad to see you, Miss!"

"They?" she said, stepping inside.

Before she could say anything more a worried Jeremy came out and took her in his arms. In an emotional voice, he exclaimed, "My dear Adele! I can't believe my eyes!"

She smiled up at him. "You see, Jeremy, I can manage some things on my own."

The dark, handsome man drew her to him and kissed her. He said, "I imagined you might be dead by now!"

"Adele!" It was Richard's voice and he came out to join them. He had a bandage wrapped around his head and looked pale and ill.

She turned from Jeremy to go to the young lawyer. "Richard! I couldn't guess what had happened to you! Why you weren't in the office!"

He grimaced. "And why the Major and that Carlos were there?"

"Yes," she said. "I walked in to your office expecting to see you and found them waiting for me instead."

Richard said, "They arrived there first. They trussed up my clerk when I was out and when I returned they struck me on the head and locked me in a closet with the bound and gagged clerk. By the time I came to, you were gone."

Jeremy said, "I came back from Scotland Yard to find you missing. Then Richard came here and told me his story and I understood."

"They took me to the house," she said.

Jeremy told her, "Richard and I were planning a raid on the place when you came back. I had my crew lined up to help us. We were going to make a last-ditch fight for you. Attack the place in strength. And you escaped on your own!"

"Not quite on my own," she said.

"Oh?" Jeremy showed interest.

Richard also stared at her. "What does that mean?"

"I was rescued by a mystery man," she said.

"Explain," Jeremy urged her.

"Do!" Richard said.

She took a deep breath. "I can't tell you much about him, except that he hates the Contessa and he knows she is a vampire."

Jeremy asked, "What else did he tell you?"

"He told me about the famous gambling casino which she operates for the Scorpion.

And he says the Contessa ruined him at the gambling tables and that he wants revenge on her."

"Where is he now?" Richard King asked.

"He left after he saw me safely here," she said.

Jeremy frowned. "Why didn't he come in with you?"

"He's a man of mystery, as I've told you," she said. "He didn't want to meet any of you."

Jeremy said, "Come inside. Richard's uncle is here. Tell us all about how your rescue was effected and all you can think of concerning this mystery man. I mean his appearance and everything about him."

"If you like," she said uneasily. She was still shaky and not too happy at the prospect of reciting her story in the presence of the famous Simon Oglethorpe.

But the imposing old man with the huge dome of a head heard her out in polite silence. And when she finished, he sighed and said, "That is a most remarkable story, Miss Foster."

Richard said, "What do you make of it, Uncle Simon?"

He waved a manicured hand. "Hard to say," he told them. "The fact that this thuggery went on in my office shakes me. The rest of it, the vampire business and all, is extraordinary!"

"Does that mean you don't believe it?" Jeremy said.

"I prefer not to commit myself about that," he said in his ponderous way. "But I will tell you what I think about this mystery man. I believe he is the Scorpion!"

Chapter Eleven

Adele was seated on a divan across from the stout old lawyer, with Jeremy seated on one side of her and Richard on the other. She heard his portentous comment on the mystery man and was at once upset.

She said, "You're wrong, Mr. Oglethorpe! I asked him if he was the Scorpion and he said no!"

Simon Oglethorpe smiled grimly. "But isn't that what you would expect him to say, Miss Foster?"

Richard nodded to her. "I think my uncle is right. It must have been the Scorpion and that is why he behaved so strangely."

Jeremy stood up and took a step away before he turned and said, "I don't think we should rush to any quick conclusions. I am inclined to agree with Adele. I don't think this man can be the Scorpion."

"Why not?" Simon Oglethorpe rasped. It was clear he didn't like his opinions questioned.

Jeremy said, "The Scorpion is behind the

Contessa. She is his puppet. Why should he rescue Adele from her?"

"That's what I say," Adele spoke up.

The stout man with the domed head eyed her with annoyance. "Young women of today are too glib with their opinions," he said tartly. "This man is a master criminal. His mind does not work like yours or mine. He could have had reasons for what he did. Probably he wanted to throw you off the track. Confuse you!"

Richard sighed. "He's surely done that!"

Jeremy said, "The important thing is that Adele was saved."

Adele looked up at him with a delightful feeling of warmth surging through her. The awful experience she had endured was almost worthwhile to hear him say this. She knew how much he wanted to avenge himself on the mysterious figure known as the Scorpion. Yet he was now willing to say this was unimportant when measured with her rescue.

She said, "Thank you, Jeremy!"

Richard looked somewhat upset. He said, "I think the important thing is to take steps against this Contessa. We can forget about this man, whoever he is. We probably will never hear from him again. I say, make a stand against the Contessa."

Jeremy nodded in agreement. "I think you are right. And it may be that we could best make war on her and her henchmen through the casino which she is operating. I hadn't thought of this until now."

"Yes," Adele said. "Since so many people enter and leave the casino it should be easier to reach her there. It is a kind of public place."

"No doubt she keeps well in the background," Jeremy mused. "But she must be there available to some of the big plungers. I assume her beauty is part of the bait to trap them into taking losses."

Richard nodded. "So we work out a campaign with the casino in mind!" He turned to his uncle. "What do you think, sir?"

The stout man had lighted a cigar and now he was puffing on it as he considered their conversation. He removed the cigar and said, "I know about this club. Very important people go there."

"The Prince of Wales goes there," Adele said.

The famous lawyer gave her a reproving look. "That is best not repeated," he warned her. "But I can tell you all the clientele is from the top layer of our society. The place is bound to have some sort of protection. I would assume that Scotland Yard looks the other way where it is concerned."

Jeremy frowned. "You're saying we daren't cause trouble for the Contessa there."

Simon Oglethorpe studied the end of his cigar. "My practice is important to me. So is my nephew's future. I would not like to place the future of our firm in jeopardy through Richard joining you in this business."

Richard stood up. "I'm sorry, Uncle, but I think we have no choice. I was attacked in my office this morning and Adele was kidnapped there. If we don't fight back where will it end?"

His uncle gave him an annoyed look. "I think it would all end quietly if Miss Foster packed her bags and went back to America. The Contessa would not bother her there."

"What about my brother?" Adele exclaimed in a hurt tone. "And his share of the estate which he left her?"

Simon Oglethorpe shrugged. "From what I have learned your brother was a rather wild young man. He was heading for some bad end before he was unfortunate enough to meet up with the Contessa. She merely hastened his ruin."

"Then you agree she brought about his death!" she said.

"I will grant that," he said. "You may think me callous but I have been in the courts a very long time. I have seen many men hang. A life as such is not all that important. Ask any famous general about that. Your brother lost his life. Why do you have to beg to have yours taken? Why bring my nephew into danger? It is different with Jeremy, he is a fanatic, of sorts. But Richard has never been involved in anything like this before. I say, Miss Foster, you should withdraw and let that rascally band have the money which you can well get along without. Go back to America and dedicate yourself to forgetting what happened here."

Adele said, "That is a most convincing argument, Mr. Oglethorpe. But I'm a girl who has lost her only brother and who has almost lost her own life. I'm sorry. I don't want Richard involved, but I can't run from the Contessa!"

Richard came over to her. "Good girl, Adele." And he turned to his uncle, who was still seated in the big easy chair. "I'm sorry, sir. But I find myself on Adele's side."

His uncle looked grim. "I expected you would be. I will not interfere. But I warn you I will not do anything to help you either. You understand that?"

"Yes, sir," Richard said, showing his disappointment in his uncle.

Simon Oglethorpe lifted himself up out of the chair with some difficulty and told them all, "I assume you would prefer that I leave since I'm not in agreement with you."

Jeremy said, "That might be best, Mr. Oglethorpe."

The old man gazed at Jeremy and shook his head. "You ruined your own practice with your melodramatics. I hope you won't ruin Richard. He is like a son to me and I have no one else to take over the firm when I am gone."

Richard said, "Don't worry about me, sir."

Adele went to the young lawyer and told him in a low voice. "Please go with your uncle. He is an old man and badly upset. Even though I disagree with him I feel sorry for him."

Richard looked at her worriedly. "You mean that?"

"Yes," she said.

"If I go now can I come back here tomorrow and take you to lunch somewhere?"

Eager for him to leave with his uncle, she decided to agree. She said, "All right. Come for me around twelve-thirty tomorrow."

"Goodnight, Adele," he said, still sounding troubled. Then he told his uncle, "I may as well leave with you, sir."

Simon Oglethorpe turned from Jeremy with whom he'd been talking and showed pleasure on his massive face. He said, "That is good of you, Richard." And to Adele he added, "Think over my advice, Miss Foster. It may seem better to you by the morning."

"I will," she promised. "But I can't see that my views will change."

The two went on their way leaving Jeremy and her alone. She and the tall, dark man sauntered back into the drawing room.

He said, "It has been a very strenuous day for us all."

"I know," she said.

Jeremy sighed. "My moving in here didn't accomplish much. You still managed to get into trouble."

"That was an unusual situation."

"Old Simon thinks you should give in and return to New York."

"Never!"

"And he says I ruined my practice for nothing!" His voice was bitter. He took out his watch and snapped the case off the back of it to stare at the photograph cut out and pasted there, of a lovely, smiling young woman. He let Adele study it. "My wife."

"She was beautiful," Adele said in a whisper. "You never let me see it before."

"I don't make a habit of exhibiting it," Jeremy said almost curtly as he snapped the watch case shut and replaced it in his pocket. "But when Simon says I wrecked my life for nothing he is very wrong."

"Of course he is," she placated him, sensing the depth of his hurt.

"Simon thinks only of himself," Jeremy said.

"He is an important man with important friends and he wishes to protect them," she said. "He is clearly afraid that some of them will be caught up in any trouble which you might cause at the casino."

"His fears will not stop my going ahead with what I have in mind," Jeremy said.

"I know you won't listen to him, nor will I," she said. "I know how evil the Contessa is and the lengths to which she will go. She has to be stopped."

"She will be," Jeremy promised. "She will be!" His handsome face was a study in grim determination as he said this.

So the night ended. To her surprise she slept better than she had for some time. And her sleep was dreamless. She felt she had been so exhausted that she had dropped off into a deep sleep the moment she'd closed her eyes.

The next day was foggy again. The fog had returned some time in the night. And it appeared that Jeremy was completing his plans because when she went down to breakfast he had already left the house. He had not given Marlow any message to pass on to her so she could only wait until he returned to find out what was taking place.

The morning went by at a dreary pace. She found herself thinking about the mystery man and she could not agree with Simon Oglethorpe's view that he was the Scorpion. She had not made up her mind about the stranger but she felt he was not the utter scoundrel that the Scorpion must be.

She couldn't help debating what the favor he might want would be? He had given her no clue to this but she guessed that whatever it was must have some great importance to him. And it was something which he couldn't do himself. It would be interesting to see if he returned as he had promised he would, to make this request of her.

As it came time to be ready to leave with Richard she went upstairs to dress. When she came downstairs in her cloak she found Marlow standing at the foot of the stairs with a concerned look on his wizened face.

She asked, "What is it, Marlow?"

The hunchback said, "Somebody standing across the street, Miss. Watching this house!"

"You're sure?"

"Look out the window for yourself!"

She crossed to the window and pulled back a curtain. And she saw that Marlow was right. Standing across the street in the shadow of a doorway was Major Merrithew. The old scoundrel was ready to make another kidnapping attempt again.

She turned from the window and told Marlow, "If Mr. Jeremy returns while I'm out with Richard King, will you please tell him about this? And if that man is still over there point him out to Jeremy."

"Yes, Miss," the old servant said.

"Tell him that is Major Merrithew," she said, naming the man across the street for his benefit.

"I will, Miss," Marlow promised.

As he said this Richard's carriage drew up before the door and he came in to get her. The moment he was inside she told him about the Major spying from across the street. Richard went to the window and stared across at the Major leaning in the doorway.

Angrily, he said, "If he dares to bother you while I'm around he'll regret it."

"He won't try anything as long as we're together," she told him. "He's waiting there on the chance of catching me going out alone."

"You mustn't ever do that until all this is settled," the young lawyer warned her.

"I know that now," she said. "Let us be on our way. And if he follows us have the cab lose him."

Richard promised he would. And when they went outside he gave the cabman instructions to that effect. But he might have saved himself the trouble since the Major made no attempt to follow them. He appeared content to keep a watch on the old mansion and the comings and goings of the people in it.

Richard took her to a new restaurant near Piccadilly Circus. It was heavily patronized at lunch and they had to wait for a table. When they finally sat down it was at a table not far from the entrance.

The young lawyer at once began to apologize. "I don't know what to say about my uncle, except that he is old and perhaps tired of the struggle."

"You mustn't worry about it," she said.

"But I do," he told her.

"Your uncle meant no harm."

"But he is too anxious to support his titled friends," the young man said. "I have decided to break away from him and start my own law practice."

She worried, "Can you hope for success on your own?"

"I see no reason why not," he said. "I'm sick of being under Uncle Simon's thumb."

"I don't want to come between you two," she protested.

Richard's young face showed worry. "Don't you care about me?"

"Of course I do."

"You're not in love with Jeremy, are you?" he asked.

The question caught her unexpectedly. She blushed and said, "Why do you ask that?"

"I must know," he said. "I find Jeremy has moved into the house with you. He kissed you so tenderly last night. I don't know whether you have fallen in love with him but I suspect he is in love with you."

"He certainly never told me that," she protested.

"I don't care," the young man said. "I have never seen Jeremy so interested in a young woman since his wife was murdered."

"I'm sure you're making much more of it than you should," she told him.

The young lawyer studied her with anguish showing on his pleasant young face. "Tell me there is a chance for me. That you have not given your heart to anyone yet?"

"Of course I haven't," she said. "And if I'm not lucky the Contessa will make certain that I never do live to marry anyone."

Richard said, "About the Contessa. I'm going to line up with Jeremy and try and drive her to the wall."

"Good," she said.

"I think the casino is the place to attack her," he went on. "We should have better luck there."

"I feel that," she agreed. "My mystery man said so."

"I wonder about him."

"I think we'll learn the truth about him soon enough," she said. "Perhaps when we have settled with the Contessa."

"You could be right," Richard agreed.

Their luncheon was a pleasant occasion. Richard saw her back to the house in his cab and they looked to see if the Major was still there spying on the house. But he had vanished.

She said happily, "Perhaps we tired him out."

Richard glanced across the street glumly. "Or he could have gone for reinforcements."

"Let us hope not," she said.

When they parted he kissed her. It was evident that he did not want Jeremy to get ahead of him. She entered the house with a small feeling of happiness. She felt as well as she could under the tragic circumstances of her losing her brother. She found Jeremy waiting for her.

He said, "You kept your luncheon appointment with Richard?"

"Yes."

Jeremy gave her a knowing glance. "I saw his parting kiss. That young man evidently has very serious notions about you."

She felt her cheeks warm. "He is very nice and he has been kind to me."

"Of course he has," Jeremy said, plainly not wanting to show any jealousy.

She sat down, and, gazing up at the tall, handsome Jeremy, said, "Had it not been for Richard I would never have met you."

Jeremy's smile was sad. "Would that have made a great difference to you?"

"Yes," she said with sincerity. "Knowing you has been one of the most important experiences of my life. I only wish we could have met under other circumstances."

"I know," he said. "But I am thankful that we met at all. The chances were slim."

"I realize that," she said. "You probably heard from Marlow that the Major was across the street this morning watching this house."

"He told me," Jeremy agreed. "And while I don't like it I think it might be of help to us. While he's there watching you he isn't helping guard the casino. And that is where we must concentrate now."

She leaned forward, all interest. "What have you found out?"

Jeremy said, "Already we know how we can get into the place."

"Good!"

"Each morning after the casino closes charwomen enter the place by a basement door and work all day cleaning the various rooms and getting it ready for the next night. Carlos supervises this work. And we have old Meg and Alfie planted among the regulars."

"That was clever," she said.

He smiled grimly. "We knew some of the regulars so it wasn't too difficult. And now when we want to enter we'll have proper keys to that door. Meg has made impressions of the locks, and the keys will be ready by tomorrow."

"Excellent," she said.

His expression became more sober. "There is something else."

She sensed he was about to offer an important revelation. She said, "Yes?"

"It is about your brother."

"What about Johnny?" she said anxiously.

"You realize that he is dead, beyond recall."

"Yes."

"And yet," Jeremy went on, "he is not at rest in his present state. He is a threat to you and a vampire puppet to be used by the Contessa as she desires."

"I know," she agreed, looking down with a tiny shudder. "It is horrible."

"You can change it."

She glanced up. "How?"

Jeremy was staring at her hard. She could tell that he was making a careful appraisal of her reactions as he said, "I now know where Johnny sleeps during the daytime hours. He is in the lower cellar at the casino. He and several others sleep there in plain box coffins."

Her eyes widened. "You've seen the coffin?"

"Yes. I have seen John asleep in it. There is one way to free him. Plant a stake in his

265

heart while he is asleep. Then he will be truly dead."

The horror of it stunned her. "That is what must be done?"

"Yes. I promise you he will feel no pain. And he will be released from his vampire bondage to the Contessa."

"Then it must be done," she said in a quiet voice.

"You will want to see him again before it is done?" Jeremy suggested.

"Yes," she said. "I would like that."

"Tomorrow afternoon we will don the rags of charwoman and dustman and join the others at the casino. We can drift unnoticed to the cellar. I will bring a proper stake and mallet with me. After you have had a glimpse of your brother I will look after the freeing of him."

"Dare we risk it?" she worried.

"We'll be disguised and perfectly safe," Jeremy said. "I want Johnny eliminated as a threat to you. And in the meantime you had better keep that crucifix close by you."

"I have the large one in my room," she told him. "The other one is lost."

Jeremy said, "I shall get you another one to wear around your neck. It could be your best protection."

"I know," she said. "It saved me before."

He went on to tell her, "Three nights from now there is to be a masquerade party at the casino. It is a yearly event. And that is the night I propose to strike against the Contessa since many of us can infiltrate the group in mask and costume. It's the ideal time to raid the place."

"Simon Oglethorpe seemed to think the police would not take any part in action against the casino since so many noted people go there."

Jeremy smiled in grim fashion. "Old Simon couldn't be more wrong. My inspector friend at Scotland Yard is ready to conduct his raid on the premises at the same time we close in on the Contessa and her associates. We are the only ones with the knowhow to deal with those evilmongers."

"I agree," she said.

"I shall want you there," Jeremy said. "And Richard. So you had best be thinking of costumes."

"I'll see to it," she said, rising. "And what about you? What do you plan to wear?"

He gave her a slightly amused look. "I will be there as Blind Paul, the beggar. I feel comfortable in that outfit."

"Be sure you're not recognized."

"The place will be crowded with people,"

he assured her. "I think we can mingle freely without being noticed."

"So it will be all settled in a few days?"

"Hopefully," he said. "Then what will you do?"

She sighed. "Return to America. I do not feel like staying here on my own."

"Must you be on your own?" Jeremy suggested.

"What else?"

"You could marry and raise a family here," Jeremy said. "England isn't all that bad."

Blushing, she said, "I like this country a great deal."

"But?"

"No one has asked me to marry them yet."

"They will," Jeremy predicted. "Wait and see."

It was a strange prediction and it made her wonder if he had in mind asking her to be his wife. She felt there was a hint of that in his manner. She both wished it might be true and worried about it. Jeremy was such a complex person she was not at all sure she could make him happy.

The balance of the day went by quickly enough. The Major came back to keep an eye on the house and remained there

watching the door until late in the afternoon. Jeremy went out on some business to
do with the projected raid on the gambling
casino which would keep him out until late
evening. So Adele was alone.

She took advantage of the time to try and
plan a costume for the masquerade which
she would attend at the casino. And she
found herself wondering about her mystery
man and whether she would see him again.
She tried to block out thoughts of the mission she and Jeremy would be going on tomorrow. They would enter the casino cellars
and she'd see her beloved brother for the
last time. After that Jeremy would pound
the stake through his heart and free him
from the vampire curse.

After dinner she busied herself again at
transforming one of her party dresses into a
sort of Spanish costume. She was in her
room working at this when old Marlow
came up and knocked on her door.

Looking up from her task, she asked,
"What is it, Marlow?"

The hunchback's wizened face showed
concern. "There is a man who wants to see
you. I wouldn't let him in until I had consulted you."

She rose. "What does he look like?"

Marlow considered, "Middle-aged and

well-dressed. His hair is iron gray and so is his mustache."

"I know him," she said. "Send him into the drawing room. I'll be down to see him in a moment."

She knew from the description it was her mystery man. And so she hurriedly checked her appearance in the dresser mirror and then went down to greet him.

He was standing waiting for her. He bowed to her and said, "Thank you for seeing me."

"I told you I would."

"Lovely ladies often forget their promises or take them lightly," he said.

"You will not find me that sort," she said.

"So I'm finding out," said the man with the face which had once been handsome.

"I worried that you mightn't make this call," she said.

"You had no reason to worry," he assured her. "Did you tell the others about me?"

"No more than you wished me to."

The man looked pleased. "I can imagine that many questions were put to you."

"Yes."

"Thank you for not betraying my confidence."

She said, "I really knew little about you to tell anyone."

The mystery man nodded. "That is the way I want it. Now we come to the reason for my seeing you again."

"Your favor?"

"Yes."

"What is it?" she asked.

In reply he produced a small black case from inside his coat and opened it to reveal a small, pearl-handled pistol. He said, "This is my personal weapon and I value it a great deal."

She stared at it. "It looks old and finely crafted."

"The weapon was made by a master craftsman on the Continent," the gray-haired man said, as he studied the weapon with affection. "I'm going to entrust it to your care."

"Why?"

"I need a set of special bullets for it," he told her. "There is only one man in London who can make them. And as I'm being spied upon I do not dare go to him. I know his shop is also being watched."

"And?"

"These people would not suspect you," he said. "So I want you to go to this shop and have the bullets made for me. Then I will call here and get them. And they must be ready by tomorrow night."

"Can they be done in that time?" she worried.

"Old Chesney can do them that fast if he likes," the gray-haired man assured her. "The shop is in Ratchet Street, number four. It's down in the cellar of a building there."

She took the case with the pistol in it. And she asked him, "How many bullets do you want and what is to be special about their construction?"

He nodded approvingly. "You have a good mind. I like the way you get to the point." And he again reached inside his coat and produced a few short pieces of what looked like wooden rods. He said, "This wood is maple of a special type. It is not available anywhere else in England. I want silver-cased bullets made with small slivers of this wood inserted in the center of them."

She stared at him. "Isn't that a bit unusual?"

"He won't think so," the gray-haired man promised her. "He has made them for me once before. And they must be crafted to work well in this pistol."

She took the pieces of wood. "When will I go see this Chesney?"

"Tonight. After I leave," he ordered her.

"Otherwise he won't be able to get the bullets done in time."

She gave him a worried look. "Will it be safe for me?"

"Take your carriage and have it wait for you," he said. "It will be all right. And I shall return here tomorrow night at nine to get my pistol and the bullets."

The mystery man left as soon as the transaction had been arranged. He also had her pledge herself to secrecy about the mission.

He warned her, "No one else must know. Not even Jeremy Quentain!"

Then as it neared ten that night she left the safety of the old mansion to drive in her carriage to Chesney Street. Marlow pleaded with her not to go out on her own but she refused to listen to him. And she found herself on her way through the dark streets on this mission of mystery and half-wondering whether or not she was heading straight into another trap!

Chapter Twelve

There was a black-lettered sign on a white board, which read: "R. Chesney, Gunsmith" outside the dingy building on narrow Ratchet Street. There were steps leading down to a cellar shop and from its murky windows there showed a faint glow of light, probably that of a candle. Adele hesitated before descending the stone steps but knew that she must make an effort to carry out the mystery man's errand.

So she went down and opened the black-painted door with its single pane of glass. A bell rang inside as she opened the door. Her first impression of the place was the odor of gunpowder mixed with fine oils. She saw a counter and the rest was shadows. From out of the shadows a bent old gnome of a man crept forward to stand behind the counter with its burning candle.

"What can I do for you, my lady?" the old man asked, gazing up at her with a crafty if rheumy eye.

"I have a commission for you," she said.

"What kind of commission?"

She produced the case with the pistol and the rods of maple wood and told him what she wanted. She said, "And the bullets must be ready by tomorrow night."

"That is impossible!" the old man protested.

"I was told it could be done," she said. "Cost is not of any importance."

The gnome's wrinkled face took on a smile. "That is different, my fine lady." And he named a large sum for the task.

She had brought along a good supply of money. And now she counted out the cash. As he took it and greedily counted it before stuffing it into a trouser's pocket, she asked him, "Can you bring the finished product to me?"

The gnome nodded. "It can be arranged. There will be an extra fee."

"I don't mind that," she told him. "I might find it hard to get back here. I'll give you my address and the pistol and bullets must be delivered before nine tomorrow night."

"You're making it difficult, fine lady," the crafty old man sighed.

"I'm paying you well," she told him sternly. "I will expect you not to be late."

He was studying the address on the scrap

of paper on which she'd written it and looking as if he wished he had charged her more. With another sigh, he said, "You can expect me around eight."

She hurried out of the shop and up the stairs to her carriage. And within a short time she was back home. Marlow was touchingly glad to see her home and safe. And she learned from him that Jeremy had not yet returned. For once she was glad of this as she hurried up to her room and to bed.

The crucifix had been hung on the wall over her bed. And that night she had dreams in which she saw her brother again. But he always remained at a distance. And when she awoke in the morning she wondered if what she'd experienced had truly been dreams or whether her brother had come back to attack her but had been kept off by the crucifix. The question disturbed her.

Jeremy had breakfast with her. He said little about what he had done except to tell her that things were moving on nicely. He said, "I also have two presents for you."

"Two?" she echoed in surprise.

He smiled thinly. "Neither of them too important," he said. "One is a ring which I want you to wear at all times." And he reached into a vest pocket and produced a ring which he gave her.

She took the ring and studied it with surprise on her lovely face. She had at first wondered if it might be a diamond engagement ring but it was something entirely different. An exquisite, carved gold ring with a tiny diamond crucifix set in it.

She said, "It's unique. I've never seen anything like it!"

Jeremy nodded. "I had a time searching it out. More practical than a hanging crucifix. You can't lose it so easily."

Adele slipped the ring on the fourth finger of her right hand and held it up for him to see. "Now I shall always be safe!"

"Don't count on it too much," he warned. "But it will surely help since it is a genuine crucifix fashioned and blessed by an Italian priest."

She smiled at him. "And what is the other gift?"

"Old clothes."

"Old clothes?" she repeated in a puzzled tone.

"The charwoman's outfit which you will wear when we go to the casino cellars this afternoon," he said.

Her face shadowed. "I'd almost forgotten."

His look was questioning. "You haven't changed your mind?"

"No," she said. "No. I realize we must go through with it."

"We leave at three," he said. "I have decided that is the best time. Meg will be there waiting for us. She will let us in."

"Very well," she said. "I'll be ready to leave when you like."

"Around two-thirty," he said. "We'll go out by the back way and walk there. Charwomen aren't able to afford carriages."

"Of course not," she agreed.

"By the way," he said. "What about your mystery man? Have you heard of him?"

"No," she said, sorry to have to lie, but knowing that she must.

Jeremy looked as if he didn't believe her but he quietly said, "Probably it is best that you haven't."

Later that afternoon when Adele had donned the charwoman's rags and stood surveying herself in her dresser mirror she knew the meaning of the phrase which said clothes make the person. She doubted that anyone would recognize her in the worn skirt and blouse with the dirty brown shawl over her head. It was an almost perfect disguise.

There was a knock on her door and she

went and opened it to see a bent, shabby man with white hair and eyebrows and a vacant, rather silly expression on his dirty face. Though she had been expecting Jeremy in disguise the striking change in his appearance came as a shock.

"I wouldn't have known you!" she gasped.

"That is the idea," he told her. "You look very well, also."

"I feel ridiculous."

"You look right," he assured her. "Now we'd best dodge out the back door before we shock Marlow or any of the other servants. It will take us a good twenty minutes walk to reach the casino."

The house in which the casino was located was a majestic one with wide marble stairs at its entrance and faces carved over its door together with mottoes in Latin. The building was in one of the fine Hyde Park locations and looked out on the lovely acres of green grass and trees. They slunk in back to a rear entrance which led to the basement and old Meg opened the door to them.

"Thought you was never going to get here," the old crone said worriedly. "They could have found me idling here and made me go back to work."

"Do that now," Jeremy said in the

shadows of the cellar. "We can do everything else on our own!"

"Watch out for that Carlos," the old
woman warned them in a hoarse whisper.
"He prowls about everywhere."

"We'll be careful," Jeremy promised.

Old Meg went back upstairs to work and
they hurried down the length of the shadowed cellar and took a short stairway down
to a level which was even lower. This was
part cellar and smaller. Jeremy had to dig
out a candle and light it to show Adele the
way.

They were arranged in a neat row there in
the dark depths, three pinewood coffins.
Jeremy went to the one at the far end and
motioned for her to join him. She was numb
with fear and her every impulse was to
shrink back. But she knew this had to be
faced. Slowly she edged over to the coffin
and looked inside to see John's pale countenance in the soft glow of the candle.

Jeremy said, "The time has come."

She nodded, her eyes blurred with tears.
She whispered, "Goodbye, Johnny!" and
she turned away with her back to the coffin.

Jeremy said nothing. But the next thing
she heard was the stake being pounded. She
listened with a chill of horror filling her.
And then there was silence. It was over!

Jeremy took her gently by the arm. "He is free at last. Now let us get safely out of here."

"Yes," she said in a broken whisper, still blinded by her tears.

They made their way up to the cellar above and were about to leave by the door through which they'd come when a sharp voice behind them called out, "You two!" It was the voice of Carlos.

Fear shot through her and she turned a little so that she caught a glimpse of the cruel associate of the Contessa over her right shoulder. Meanwhile, Jeremy, playing his role as the bent old cleaning man, halted and made a simpering bow to the irate, white-haired Carlos.

"Yes, sir," he said in a silly, frightened voice.

"You two have been taking time off!" Carlos said sharply, moving a step towards them.

"Only a few minutes, your honor. We won't do it again!"

"I promise you that you won't," Carlos said. "You're both of you discharged! Get out!"

She was delighted to hear his words and ready to leave but Jeremy held back. Holding out a hand, he asked forlornly, "What about our money, your honor?"

"You don't get a sou!" Carlos told him angrily. "Now get out of my sight, both of you, before I really lose my temper!"

"Yes, your honor," Jeremy quavered.

He came to her and in a frightened manner took her arm and urged her on her way. Within a few minutes they were out of the cellar and safe.

Jeremy gave her a glance. "That was close!"

"I know," she said. "I was sure he'd recognize us. I almost died."

"I could tell you were nervous," Jeremy agreed.

"What now?" she asked.

"Get away from here as quickly as we can," Jeremy said.

They went directly home and in the rear way again. Soon she was out of the ragged outfit and dressed for dinner. They were expecting Richard King and she wanted to look her best.

Richard arrived full of talk about setting up his own office. He told her, "I have a location just across the street from where I am now. And I think I'll prosper on my own."

"I hope so," she said wanly. "I feel responsible for this move you're making."

"Not at all," Richard said. "It is something I should have done long ago only I couldn't find the courage. This situation brought the whole business to a head."

Jeremy had joined them and he said, "I'd say your Uncle Simon is too conservative. He probably has been holding you back."

"I feel that way," the young lawyer said. "I hope I can prove it."

She anxiously asked him, "Are you certain you wish to join us?"

"I am," Richard said.

Adele turned to Jeremy, "Shall I tell him?"

"Yes," Jeremy said. "I suppose so." But he warned the young lawyer, "Not a word of what Adele tells you to anyone. And since your uncle has so many friends in high places, especially not to your uncle."

"Have no worries on that score," Richard said. "He's angry with me and we aren't speaking."

She quickly explained what they had planned and ended with, "Scotland Yard is going to call a raid while the masked ball is on. That should just about finish the Contessa's profitable game."

"It sounds as if it would work," Richard said.

Jeremy shrugged. "Some details need completing. And there is the likelihood we'll never get a whisper about the Scorpion who is really the one behind the gambling operation. He makes use of creatures like the Contessa."

Richard was standing between her and Jeremy and he said, "But let us remember that Adele's quarrel is with the Contessa. You are the one out to settle with the Scorpion."

Jeremy suddenly looked dejected. "You are right. I suppose I occasionally forget that. Thank you for reminding me."

Adele felt upset and she at once turned to the handsome, dark-haired man and said, "After what you've done for me, your enemy is my enemy. I feel just as strongly about this Scorpion as you do!"

Jeremy brightened. "Thank you, dear Adele," he said quietly.

She was relieved when Jeremy announced that he must go out for an hour after dinner. He claimed it was to see some of his renegade group who would be helping him the night of the raid. He took Richard along with him so she was left alone. This was exactly what she wanted since she was expecting callers.

The gnomelike gunsmith arrived shortly after eight. Marlow let him in with a look of distaste on his wizened face. She took the package with the gun and bullets and examined it to make sure everything was there. It was! There were six shining silver bullets.

"A rush order, fine lady," the bent old gunsmith whined. "You owe me another five sovereigns!"

She paid him and he left, bowing and scraping, and telling her that any other time she needed something in his line not to hesitate coming to see him. She was relieved when the door closed after him since he was not a person in whom she felt any trust.

The mystery man arrived an hour later. He was barely inside the house when he asked her, "Did you get the bullets?"

"Yes," she said. She went and got them for him.

Eagerly he opened the case and checked the pearl-handled pistol and the silver bullets. His once-handsome face was radiant as he looked up from them. He said, "You did not fail me."

"I always try to keep my word," she said.

He nodded. "You are a person of integrity. I like that."

"May I ask you a question?" she said.

He smiled thinly. "I suppose you are entitled to one."

"What do you plan to do with those bullets?"

"Game, my dear. I plan to do some

hunting. And I required ammunition of exactly the right sort."

"You're a sportsman, then?"

"Yes. You could call me that."

"And you are not English, are you?" she said. "It's another question, but I can detect a slight accent."

The mystery man seemed amused. "I thought over the years I had lost any accent. But you are right. I was not born in England. Still, it is my home now."

"I see," she said. "Will we ever meet again?"

The mystery man's time-ravaged face showed thought. "That is a difficult question. I would think that we wouldn't. Still, it is a small world. You never can be sure."

"I hope we do," she said. "I think you are rather nice. And I wish you good hunting."

The mystery man bowed. "Thank you, Miss Foster. May I say I have much enjoyed our meeting and I wish you well in all things."

He left immediately after that and she watched him walk off into the darkness and vanish. Somehow she felt she would see him again, that one day he might again play some important role in her life.

She was still sitting in the drawing room by the fireplace when Jeremy returned.

Wearing his dark cloak and deerstalker hat, he came in to stand by her.

He asked her, "Isn't it unusual for you to be up this late?"

She smiled up at him. "I was waiting for you."

"I'm flattered," he said, removing his hat and cloak and placing them on a nearby chair. He stood smiling at her. "May I suggest a sherry?"

"I'd like one," she said.

He poured a glass of sherry for each of them and came over with hers. He raised his own glass. "To our success."

"Yes," she said, raising her glass and then sipping the sherry.

"If we are successful I will be leaving here," he reminded her. "I shall miss you."

"And I shall miss you," she said. "What about Richard? Was he any help to you tonight?"

"That young man is extremely tense," Jeremy frowned. "I think breaking with his uncle was more difficult for him than he would have us believe."

"I suspected that," she said.

Jeremy asked her, "Were you bothered in any way during my absence?"

"No," she said. "It has been quite quiet for a change."

"I suspect that condition won't last long," he said dryly. "The Contessa will be enraged when John does not appear tonight and she knows that she has lost him."

"Yes, that will anger her," she said quietly. "But at least we know that tonight Johnny is finally at rest."

"Yes," Jeremy said, finishing his sherry.

She looked up at him. "When this case is finished, will you go back to that cottage in Fetter Lane where I first called on you?"

"Where else?" he said. "It is my home."

"But you live the life of a recluse there!"

"I enjoy quiet living," he said.

Adele got to her feet. "There are so many legends about you. Some say that you take drugs."

"They are entitled to their opinion," Jeremy said with a wry look.

Her eyes met his and she asked him, "Will you ever be truly happy again, Jeremy? Able to forget about her?"

His answer was to gently take her in his arms and smile down at her in a manner he never had before. He said, "May I tell you, dear Adele, that you have brought me as close to that kind of happiness as I have ever been since that tragic night."

She stared at him. "But not far enough?"

"I can't say at this point," he told her. "Let

us see what happens on Thursday night. If I should discover the Scorpion's identity and know him to be dead, I might feel entirely different."

"I see," she said. "Then we can only wait."

"Yes," he said intently. And he drew her lips to his and kissed her tenderly. Then he saw her up to her bedroom door and bade her goodnight.

The period which followed was a tense one. And by the time Thursday evening arrived Adele's nerves were drawn to the point of breaking.

She had transformed her dress into that of a Spanish lady, and with a black wig and mask she felt sure she would be reasonably safe at the casino. Richard was wearing a seventeenth century French cavalryman's uniform which he had found in a family trunk. This, with the white powdered wig of the period was sufficient disguise for him. And Jeremy had donned the rags and black spectacles of Blind Paul.

They took a carriage to the casino and left it some little distance from the imposing building. It was after ten o'clock and the revelry was just beginning. Fine carriages and hired cabs were driving up at the front entrance of the casino and depositing their passengers at the front door. Jeremy's trio elected to enter by the rear door, using the keys which Meg had secured for them. And once inside the building they went up to the main lobby and mingled with the others.

The huge, high-ceilinged room was so crowded with masked people in various masquerade costumes that Adele was certain none of them would be recognized. Champagne was flowing like water, and there were tables laden with the finest of foods. A great fountain in the center of the room sent sprays of colored water up into the air.

The room had been decorated with gay flags and ribbons and special lanterns had been strung overhead. An orchestra played waltzes vigorously in one corner of the big room and a number of couples were dancing.

Jeremy whispered in her ear, "The gambling rooms are mostly upstairs. And that is where we will find the Contessa and her cohorts."

Behind her fan, she said, "We should be up there when the raid begins, shouldn't we?"

"Yes," Jeremy said. "Otherwise she and some of the others close to her might elude the police."

Richard King asked, "Is the raid due soon?"

"Not for a while yet," Jeremy told him.

Richard smiled at her, his mask hiding the upper half of his face, as he said, "Then let us enjoy a waltz or two!"

Before she could protest he had taken her out onto the floor. The music was excellent and the company gay but she felt like anything but waltzing. This was to be a night of reckoning, the night when she hoped to avenge the cruel murder of her brother. However, she had no choice. Richard waltzed her around the floor until the musicians paused for a moment.

Breathlessly, he said, "That was delightful."

She heard him but her eyes were fixed on the marble stairway which led from the gambling rooms. Standing near the top of the broad winding stairs and watching the revelers below were three figures whom she instantly recognized. She turned and tapped the young lawyer on the arm with her fan.

"Look up there," she told him. "The gypsy woman, the Moorish servant and the Union Army officer. Do you know them?"

"Of course," he said, staring up at the trio. "Despite their masks I'd know them anywhere. That's the Contessa, Carlos and the Major. You could count on the Major wearing a military uniform!"

"Now they're going back up again," she said, watching as the three vanished at the decorated landing. Turning to him, she suggested, "We'd better join Jeremy and make our way up there gradually. The raid can't be all that far off now."

"I agree," he said. And he guided her back through the clusters of celebrating masqueraders. They found Jeremy in his costume of Blind Paul standing alone near the fountain.

Jeremy at once greeted them with, "I'm glad you're back. We must go upstairs. It is getting near the zero hour!"

"I thought so," she said. "What do you have in mind for the Contessa?"

Jeremy said, "I haven't decided yet. I can't imagine that placing her in a prison cell will help much."

Richard said, "She'd be liable to transform herself into a bat and escape. They say these vampire people can do that."

"I will warn the inspector," Jeremy said. "If he can keep her in custody until morning, and the other vampires as well, she will go into the death state again. When they see that change in her they will know."

All three of them joined with a few people who were going upstairs for some gambling. Adele heard discussions of the roulette table above and the high stakes that were played around it. They reached the upper level and followed the others into the large room with the roulette table in its center under a brightly lighted crystal chandelier. A fairly large group was gathered at the table while the Contessa, flanked by Carlos and the Major, stood a little way behind the croupier.

The Contessa was chatting amiably with a bald man in a monk's habit. Adele and Jeremy went up to the roulette table and watched the game for a few moments while Richard took a stand on the other side of the table, almost directly across from them.

The croupier called for new bets and Adele glanced back at the Contessa and suddenly became aware that the woman was watching her!

Adele touched Jeremy's arm and whispered, "I think she has recognized us. I can see her eyes fixed on me behind the mask."

"You're probably imagining it," he said, not looking at the Contessa.

"I don't think so!" she worried.

But she never did find out for certain. At that moment there was an uproar from downstairs and she knew the raid had begun. The sounds of the raucous voices announcing the raid below caused a panic upstairs. The croupier at once vanished and the players at the roulette table scattered through the room in an attempt to escape.

Adele remained with Jeremy by the table and saw the Contessa coming towards them in a menacing fashion. Carlos and the Major were close behind her!

And then the unexpected! From behind them somewhere a figure in the black costume of Satan with his face and head covered by a black mask and headpiece appeared. He planted himself directly before the Contessa and drew a pearl-handled pistol from his pocket.

"Very well, Maria!" he shouted.

The Contessa halted and shrank back. "You!" she cried.

Carlos came quickly up to her and staring at the man said, "It can't be!"

"It is," the masked man gloated. "Luigi!" And he fired directly into the Contessa's heart, then he shot at Carlos and felled the big white-haired man. The Major turned to flee and he received a bullet between his shoulders. A great red stain showed there and he fell forward on his face.

The Contessa was writhing on the floor in pain and an eerie transformation was taking place. Her lovely face, the mask torn aside in her agonies, was aging by the second. She became an old withered creature as they watched. When she finally became still in death her face was gray, wrinkled, and her body appeared likely to disintegrate to dust and bones when she was touched. Later this did happen.

But now the Satan figure held them spellbound as he put the silver pistol to his temple and pulled the trigger. The bullet found its place in his skull and he fell to the floor, a suicide.

The few left in the room were shouting and screaming and this, added to the pandemonium from downstairs, made a weird chorus to accompany the three murders and the suicide.

Jeremy bent down and removed the Satan mask from the man who'd just killed himself, and revealed was the face of the mystery man. But he was also changing quickly, his face withering and becoming a pale gray.

"That's my mystery man!" she cried, standing back from him.

Jeremy got up and turned to her solemnly. "He was a vampire also. Did you guess that?"

"No," she said. "He seemed quite normal to me."

"But you only saw him at night," Richard King chimed in. "So you wouldn't know."

Jeremy took her by the arm. "Let us get

downstairs. I have to speak to the Inspector and this scene of slaughter isn't any place for you."

"I agree," she said weakly, hardly conscious that it was all over, that her mystery man had done their work for them.

Later, when she and Jeremy and Richard returned to her house, they put the pieces all together. In the meantime Jeremy had found some identification papers on the man of mystery.

Seated before a blazing log fire with Jeremy standing by the fireplace and Richard sitting on the arm of her chair, she asked the handsome, dark man, "Who was he?"

Jeremy smiled. "Luigi? None other than Count Luigi Fillipio. The husband of Contessa Maria. The one who created her and made her a vampire in the first place."

Adele said, "But long ago you told me that Carlos became the Contessa's lover and destroyed the Count. You said Carlos put a stake through his heart!"

"He didn't do a thorough job," Jeremy said. "Count Luigi recovered and from then on his one thought was revenge. He got it tonight."

Richard spoke with disappointment. "I hoped this mystery man might be the Scorpion."

Jeremy shook his head. "I'm afraid not. As usual the Scorpion let his underlings pay the price while he drew back into the shadows to hide. It will take another time to deal with him."

"The danger for you is over," Jeremy said. "Your enemy was the Contessa. You need worry no more."

When it came time for Richard to say goodnight and leave she accompanied him to the door. She could see that the young lawyer was upset.

In a low voice he said, "What about Jeremy? Will you and he plan some future together?"

"I doubt it," she said.

"I hope not," Richard said impulsively. "You know I love you and I want to marry you." And rather clumsily he took her in his arms and kissed her goodnight. Then he left hurriedly.

She found herself embarrassed and somewhat stunned. She was fond of Richard, but there was Jeremy. And in the tall, handsome former lawyer she felt she had found everything she could wish for in a man.

She strolled slowly back to the drawing room where Jeremy still stood by the fireplace. Jeremy's eyes fixed on her and he said, "Richard asked you to be his wife, didn't he?"

She hesitated, then said, "Yes."

"I thought he would," Jeremy sighed. "Well, we can talk about that later. Time for bed now." He accompanied her upstairs and at her door, halted and kissed her goodnight. Then he said, "You and I have had a special understanding. You realize that, don't you?"

"Yes," she said softly. He kissed her again and then walked down the corridor into the darkness.

It was the last time she was to see him. When she went down to breakfast in the morning Jeremy Quentain had left. At her place there was an envelope addressed to her. Tears brimming in her eyes, she sat limply in her chair and opened it. The message was brief.

"My Dearest Adele, It is better this way. Parting could be so painful to both of us. I am not ready for your love so it must be Richard, mustn't it? He's a fine young man. You'll both be very happy. *Au revoir,* Jeremy."

So he was lost to her. Gone back to that cottage in Fetter Lane to live the solitary life he'd known before. There he would wait until someone else came to him in distress and he roused himself from the lethargy of his small world to help them. And always he would be on the lookout for the Scorpion and that final moment of settlement!

She went to the window and saw the fog had returned again. It was another bleak day. And she knew Jeremy was right, she would marry Richard King and they would have a happy life. But always in the secret depths of her heart there would be a small area reserved for Jeremy. As a presence he had vanished, but his spirit would remain with her forever.

We hope you have enjoyed this Large Print book. Other Thorndike, Wheeler or Chivers Press Large Print books are available at your library or directly from the publishers.

For more information about current and up-coming titles, please call or write, without obligation, to:

Publisher
Thorndike Press
295 Kennedy Memorial Drive
Waterville, ME   04901
Tel. (800) 223-1244

Or visit our Web site at:
www.gale.com/thorndike
www.gale.com/wheeler

OR

Chivers Large Print
published by BBC Audiobooks Ltd
St James House, The Square
Lower Bristol Road
Bath BA2 3SB
England
Tel. +44(0) 800 136919
email: bbcaudiobooks@bbc.co.uk
www.bbcaudiobooks.co.uk

All our Large Print titles are designed for easy reading, and all our books are made to last.